FLEA THE SCENE

A WHISKERS AND WORDS MYSTERY
BOOK THREE

ERYN SCOTT

KRISTOPHERSON
PRESS
Publishing

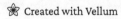

Everyone in town is *buttoned up* about the truth behind the mysterious mansion on Thread Lane.

Louisa (Lou) Henry can't seem to get any answers about the abandoned mansion hidden behind brush that she runs by each day. Well, she thought it was abandoned, but she's recently seen signs of life. Whenever she asks the locals about who lives there, they clam up.

One day, Lou notices someone sneaking around the mysterious house. When she hears a crash inside, she runs to help. The body of a man lies inside, unconscious. As Lou arrives on the scene, someone else is leaving in a hurry. Lou stays with the man only to find he's already dead, and realizes she might've just let his murderer run free.

As Lou investigates what happened, she uncovers the reason behind the man's secluded status, as well as a heap of suspects who would've wanted him dead. Can she parse the truth from the decades of lies?

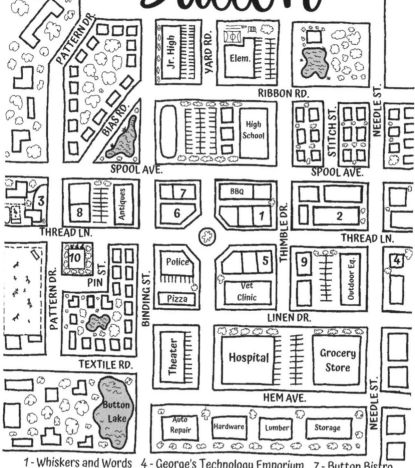

Welcome to Button

1 - Whiskers and Words   4 - George's Technology Emporium   7 - Button Bistro
2 - Material Girls   5 - Bean and Button Coffeehouse   8 - Pet Store   9 - Bakery
3 - Willow and Easton's houses   6 - The Upholstered Button   10 - Old Mansion

CHAPTER 1

L ouisa Henry loved the way her mind turned off whenever she was on a run. Even the most consuming, difficult thoughts shifted quietly to the background as she ran.

She knew this wasn't the case for everyone. In fact, her late husband, Ben, used to go on runs specifically to think through problems. He'd pull on his running shoes, stick in earbuds, kiss her cheek—his scratchy beard rough against her skin—and say, *"By the time I get back, I'll have this figured out."* And he always would.

Lou, however, didn't enjoy listening to music, audiobooks, or podcasts while she ran. She preferred to listen to the sounds around her. She loved the rhythmic crunch of her shoes on pavement or a pebbled pathway and how the birdsong in the park could drown out the sounds of traffic in the city.

Her detail-focused mind latched on to the sensory smorgasbord that surrounded her, replacing her day-to-day thoughts and worries. Instead of obsessing about the book she was currently editing, she studied a melodic birdsong. Running through a cloud of clean cottony steam coming from a laundry vent never reminded her of the laundry she had to do at home. Consuming thoughts about a leaking sink were drowned out by people-watching. She loved making up backstories for the people or buildings she ran by regularly.

As lovely as she'd found running through Central Park during her time living in New York City, her new town of Button, Washington—though small—provided ample sights and sounds to keep her occupied. There were still people to watch, but now she didn't have to fabricate life stories for strangers.

After six months in the tiny town, she knew most of the locals, along with many details about their lives. She knew which houses belonged to whom, and she'd heard the stories behind the more interesting Button buildings. Birds' songs were abundant here—especially on a warm summer morning like this one—and Lou knew which houses might have a cat sunning on the front porch or a dog running along the fence line. She passed by fields of cows and horses and witnessed adorable scenes like a real squirrel examining a ceramic squirrel in someone's garden.

Speaking of gardens, the people of Button were proud of their yards, boasting gardens that were feasts for her eyes. Flowers of every variety, yard ornaments made from recycled glass bottles and twisted wire, cement statues, pond features, and hidden pathways were in abundance.

All of it was delightfully distracting.

And Lou especially needed the distraction today. Today would've been Ben's thirty-eighth birthday. It was the first of his birthdays she'd had to endure without him since he passed away last summer from a sudden heart attack, and she was having a harder time than she'd expected.

For the first time in a while, Lou couldn't push her thoughts to the background while she ran. Everything she noticed on her run seemed to be concentrated around Ben, bringing up thoughts and memories of him.

Ben would've laughed at that garden sign that said, "Loam wasn't built in a day," she thought as she ran by a charming yard.

Oh, look. What a beautiful nasturtium. Ben brought home one of those once. It was the only plant he'd ever killed, she mused while appreciating the orange blooms in a window flower box.

Ben was fascinated by huge, Victorian-style houses like this one, Lou thought as she slowed to a stop in front of the mysterious building on Thread Lane.

Ever since she'd moved to Button, the decrepit house had drawn her attention. The mansion was like a poorly worded sentence in a manuscript from her former life as an editor at a New York publishing house. It was not as easily addressed as an obvious typo. The house on Thread Lane was a conundrum, like a sentence that begged to be read and reread until she figured out what issue was drawing her attention.

It was also the only building in Button that Lou hadn't heard about from the locals. No one talked about it, actually. Which only made it all the more intriguing to Lou.

The mansion was three stories, but even with its enormous size, it hid, almost successfully, behind towering bamboo plants and a small forest of fir trees growing ever closer to its dilapidated exterior walls. It was unclear whether the peeling brown paint had been the original color of the house or if the paint had degraded to that shade over the years. A moss-covered roof was missing more than a few shingles, and led Lou to believe the interior would smell musty and damp during the rainy months of the year.

It was so run-down, so abandoned, that Lou had, at first, assumed the place was uninhabited. But little things over the past few months had brought that into question. She'd spied a light on inside, a window sash opened just a few inches to let in the air, and a potted plant sitting on the porch.

Someone lived in the house; Lou was sure of it. And today she saw an opportunity to figure out who.

Up ahead on the sidewalk, bustling toward her, was an old woman whom Lou passed by frequently on her runs. The woman walked every day it seemed. She wore a clear plastic coat, even when it wasn't raining, and used a walking stick to help her along. The effect created was a squeaky, lopsided gait that was unmistakable.

Lou had yet to learn the woman's name, but they'd waved at each other enough times that Lou felt confident she wouldn't come off as creepy if she asked her a question. In her experience, the people of Button loved nothing more than to prove how well they knew their town and the people who inhabited it.

Pretending to catch her breath as she waited for the old woman to come closer, Lou studied the large house. The *shuffle-click-shuffle-click* of the elderly woman and her cane drew closer and Lou smiled.

"Beautiful day out," Lou said.

The old woman nodded and returned the smile.

"You don't happen to know who lives in this house, do you?" Lou asked as she gestured to the mansion.

The woman didn't even glance in the house's direction before saying, "I don't see a house over there." She continued walking.

Lou blinked, confusion wrapping around her. She pointed at the house and was about to say something else, when she realized the old woman had changed her normal gait, speeding up so much that she was practically running away.

Narrowing her eyes, Lou studied the intriguing house for a few more seconds before moving on and continuing her run.

Lou's mind was still buzzing with questions about the mysterious mansion when she arrived back at the bookstore she owned, Whiskers and Words.

Now, questions about the old woman were mixed in with her queries about the mansion. Was the woman's vision bad? Did she really not see the house? Maybe the old woman didn't wear her glasses while she was out walking. Lou pondered the options as she walked through the quiet bookshop.

Heading up the staircase at the back of the building, Lou entered the two-bedroom apartment she lived in above the shop. She loved these summer days when the sun rose early enough for her to go for a jog before she opened. After showering and making herself breakfast, Lou made the trip back down the stairs. But she wasn't alone on the walk down the staircase to the bookshop below. A small herd of cats darted around and in front of her feet, and one lagged just behind her. She greeted each feline as they assembled by the door leading into the bookshop.

"Purrt Vonnegut, first to the door, as always." She scratched the head of a lovable orange cat before opening the door and watching him slip through.

"See you tonight, Catnip Everdeen," Lou called after an orange-and-white cat who slunk through the opening and immediately disappeared behind a bookshelf. The cat was a master at hiding.

Lou bent down to stroke the soft gray fur of a beautiful tabby. "Anne Mice, you are so very nice." She chuckled at the rhyme as the cat, satisfied with the attention, strolled into the shop.

And then there was one cat left at Lou's feet, curling around her calf and rubbing his face on her leg. She stooped down to pick up the white cat with brilliant blue eyes.

"Morning, Sapphire." She kissed the top of his head and scrunched her fingers into his dense alabaster fur. A contented purr rumbled from his throat as he pushed his forehead into her chin. His paws kneaded into her shoulder, and when she tried to put him down, he clung on to her.

This was odd. Her independent cat was usually content to go off and find a sunbeam to nap in once she greeted him in the morning, but today was different. His jewel-toned eyes locked on to hers, and he bumped his head into her again.

"Oh, Sapphy. You know, don't you?" Lou hugged the cat closer. She adjusted the collar around his neck that had the words *not for adoption* printed along its length.

Unlike the other cats in Whiskers and Words, Sapphire was in his forever home. While the others had come to her over the past few months because they needed a place to stay until they were adopted, Sapphire had been with her since he'd been a tiny ball of white fluff. She and Ben had picked him out years ago, excited to give the small, deaf kitten a forever home among the books and plants of their Manhattan condo. He would be the unofficial mascot of the bookstore they would open together one day, whenever they tired of the constant grind of working as an editor and a professor, living in the city that never sleeps.

Well ... part of that dream had come true, but as sweet as the reality of Lou's dream bookshop was, Ben's absence was something she would never get used to. After all, even one missing piece of a puzzle could make the picture incomplete.

Sapphire must've had some sort of cat sense that Lou needed a little extra love today. She wouldn't have put it past Sapphy to have actually realized it was Ben's birthday either; the cat always had such a strong connection with him.

Lou carried Sapphy as she walked forward into the bookshop. Cats skittered around her feet as Lou poured fresh food into their bowls. She set Sapphy next to his bowl of food and went to open the shop door. An old man paced out front, a newspaper tucked under one arm, a bowler hat sitting atop his head. He furrowed his fluffy gray eyebrows as he checked his watch.

Lou grinned. There were still three minutes to go before eight, but she turned the lock anyway.

"Morning, Silas," she said, pulling open the door and holding it so he could enter.

The man grumbled out a hello and ambled past her to his normal spot in the tweedy gray armchair.

Louisa didn't mind that Silas came in each day and read a newspaper in her shop instead of a book. He'd purchased many books from her since she'd opened, but the man's true value lay in the attention he provided to the cats. He loved the animals but wasn't allowed to have any in his assisted-living apartment. So he came in daily to get his fix, and the shop cats got some of the love they all deserved, especially Catnip Everdeen.

The shy orange-and-white feline slunk over to Silas and crawled into his lap, pawing distractedly at the crinkly newspaper he held. If Silas didn't show up, Lou wouldn't see Catnip all day. But the otherwise introverted feline loved that old man. He was the one person who could pull her out of her hiding spots.

Speaking of visitors for the cats, the next person through the front door of the bookshop was a young woman named George. She owned a tech store down the street and had taken to coming in daily, like Silas, but didn't even pretend to care about reading or books. The twentysomething was more interested in video games and Dungeons and Dragons, and even though she would purchase a speculative fiction or fantasy

7

novel sporadically, the books weren't what drew her to the store each day. She simply flopped onto the floor, waiting for the cats to encircle her, and chatted with Lou.

"Annie's fur is extra shiny today." George smiled as Anne Mice and Purrt Vonnegut walked circles around her. They purred as she ran her hands over their backs and tails.

"I'll let Marigold know that all her brushing is paying off," Lou said, mentioning the nine-year-old daughter of Noah, the local veterinarian, and Cassidy, a real estate agent.

During the summer, Marigold had been spending a lot more of her time with Lou at the bookstore, and even had a standing appointment on Friday at four after her softball practice to come brush the cats while she waited for her mom to finish up with her work for the day. Lou had told her not to come today, of course, knowing she would need space for Ben's birthday.

Lou's last daily visitor wandered in a few moments later, holding his usual coffee. Forrest was a local psychologist and a cat lover who lived with an allergic spouse. He nodded a hello at everyone before settling onto the love seat with a book. Forrest barely patted the cushion next to him before Anne Mice, the gray tabby, left George and was by his side.

Once Silas, George, and Forrest were settled, Lou cleared her throat. They glanced up—as did a few of the cats.

"I had a weird experience this morning on my run," Lou began. When she was met with the interested expressions of her regulars, she said, "I stopped to catch my breath in front of that old mansion on Thread Lane." She watched them closely.

At the mention of the house, Silas frowned, George focused on petting the cats, and Forrest picked at the hem of his shirt.

"And the woman who walks around in a plastic coat passed by," Lou continued.

"Delores," Forrest offered.

Lou nodded. "Delores walked by. I asked her if she knew

who lived there, and she pretended not to see the house. That *enormous* house," Lou scoffed.

But if Lou was hoping for someone to share in her exasperation, she was disappointed. Forrest busied himself by taking a long gulp of his coffee, Silas muttered something unintelligible, and George quietly said, "Delores has poor eyesight."

Lou folded her arms. "And now all of *you* are acting weird about it too. Who lives there?" she asked, earnestness tightening her tone.

"I, uh, have to go," George said. Both her posture and tone were tight with discomfort. She stood and was out the door before Lou could even say goodbye.

"What was that about?" Lou asked.

Silas snorted. "Just leave it alone."

But Lou's gaze focused on the front door George had just rushed through. "Did I upset her by bringing up the person who lives in that house?"

"How are you sure someone lives there?" Silas asked, his eyes only flicking to meet hers before they moved back to his paper.

"It's very run-down. It definitely looks like no one lives there." Forrest wouldn't even meet Lou's gaze, instead focusing on his name scrawled across the side of his coffee cup.

"But someone does. I've seen signs." Lou glared at them, sure they were hiding something.

"Lou, believe us, you do not want to get involved with that house," Forrest said. "I wouldn't ask questions about it or even worry about it. Take Delores's lead and pretend it doesn't exist. You'll thank us." With that, Forrest opened his book, signaling an end to the conversation.

Lou tapped her fingers on the countertop in front of her. Forrest's warning to leave it alone only increased her interest in the house.

If she'd learned one thing about the townspeople of Button, it was that they loved to tell stories, no matter how personal, no matter how scandalous. George's quick departure after Lou brought up the mansion only added to the intrigue.

Now Lou *had* to know the secrets it held within its decrepit walls.

CHAPTER 2

The rest of the day sped by as Lou obsessed over the mysterious mansion. Focusing on the local mystery turned out to be a break from thoughts of Ben's birthday. While she'd expected the day to be difficult, it was turning out to be even harder than she'd imagined, and she was grateful for the distraction researching the mansion on Thread Lane created.

She tried looking online, hoping to find information on the property, but it was as if the whole of the internet was included in Button's moratorium on giving out information about the mansion. The only thing she could find was a sales date on a real estate website, showing the house had sold about thirty years prior. So whoever lived there—and Lou was convinced someone did—had owned the home for a long time.

Once Forrest and Silas left, Lou tried her luck getting information out of different locals who stopped by the shop throughout the day. And though she was hopeful someone would tell her the truth, she was met with more of the same avoidance.

"Oh, don't you bother yourself about that old place."

"I barely notice there's a house there anymore."

"Nothing good comes out of talking about that house."

Even Lou's best friend, Willow, was unhelpful when she stopped by after lunch.

"That place?" Willow had wrinkled her nose. "I always figured it was abandoned."

Lou held back a groan of frustration. "You've never heard the locals talk about it?"

While not a lifelong citizen of Button, Willow had lived there for close to a decade, and owned the house kitty-corner from the mysterious mansion. Lou had hoped her friend would have at least some information about the place.

But Willow shook her head. "No one talks about it."

"Don't you think that's strange?" Lou opened her hands, palms up.

Willow squinted one eye. "I suppose. I guess I always figured someone died there, or something bad happened that they want to forget."

It was during times like these that Lou really wished her friend cared about details as much as she did. But there was no changing Willow.

"George left really quickly after I brought up the house," Lou said, straightening books on the shelf in front of her.

"I've never seen George upset about anything." Willow shrugged.

"Well, her grandparents raised her. She might have a difficult past." Lou pulled out a book, glanced at the cover, and then returned it to the shelf.

Willow inclined her head. "True. Come to think of it, I've never heard the story behind George's parents and why they weren't around."

"So the town's being tight-lipped about that too." Lou narrowed her eyes.

Proving Lou was the only one still thinking about the mysterious mansion, Willow asked, "Any requests for tonight?" She scooped Anne Mice into her arms and cuddled the cat.

Lou's lips tugged up into a smile. Willow had offered to have her over tonight for dinner. And even though the two best friends shared meals together more often than not throughout the week, Lou knew her friend was trying to soften the emotional blow brought on by Ben's birthday as much as she could.

"How about that Thai peanut salad?" Lou suggested, knowing it was one of Willow's favorite meals to make.

Willow nodded. "That sounds great."

"What time should I come over? And what can I bring?" Lou asked, waving to greet a customer as they walked through the bookshop door.

"Just bring yourself around ... six-ish?" Willow tilted her hand back and forth as if to signify her unsteady relationship with time.

Lou suppressed a chuckle. "Okay."

At the best of times, Willow wasn't as punctual as Lou. She had the tendency to get lost in chores around her small farm, messing with the plants in her garden, or tending to her horse and his goat companion. But during summer days, free from the confines of her job as a high school horticulture teacher, Willow leaned in and seemed to forget about the concept of time all together. *Barn Time,* as she called the phenomenon that happened when she was with her horse—hours becoming like mere minutes—became her only sense of time.

Willow set down the cat she held. "Hang in there. I'll see you tonight." Before leaving, Willow lunged toward Lou and pulled her into a fierce hug. Then she was out the door.

Lou exhaled, watching her friend go, the tightness in her chest loosening just a little.

Even though the bookstore was busy the rest of the day, Lou couldn't help but let her thoughts drift back to the mansion on Thread Lane. Curiosity built in her like a hunger. She could feel it between her shoulder blades, like an itch in the middle of her back that she couldn't quite reach.

Lou knew she would have to pass by the mansion again when she walked over to Willow's for dinner. The need to stop and study the house in more detail clawed at her, and she tried to think of a plan that would help her do just that. She could pretend to tie her shoelace as she studied the house. What if she faked having a cramp in her leg that needed to be stretched right there? She wrinkled her nose. That plan would work better if she was out on a run instead of walking to Willow's for dinner.

Eventually, she settled on a plan that involved her acting as if she'd gotten a text message in order to take out her phone and snap a quick picture of the place. That way she could study it in private without appearing so suspicious.

Plan in place, excitement filled Lou as she locked up and headed over to Willow's that evening. It was one of those summer evenings that just seems to put everyone in a fantastic mood. The sun was shining, birds were chirping, and it was warm enough outside that Lou had only brought a light jacket for her walk home later that night.

She took a right down Thread Lane from the bookshop's front door and walked down the bustling sidewalks. She passed by the ice cream parlor next door and glanced at the confections on display in the windows of the candy shop on the corner before crossing Binding Street and the roundabout in the center of downtown.

Lights were still on in the antique shop farther down the road even though it technically closed at the same time as the bookshop each day. The owner, Smitty, often got to talking to customers and lost track of time.

Crossing the street so she would be on the same side as the mansion, Lou slowed her pace.

She could've won an Oscar for the acting she did to pretend she'd gotten a message on her phone. Staring at the screen, she poked at the icons until her camera app opened. She clicked a quick picture and was about to take another when her lips parted in surprise as she caught a movement in one of the upstairs windows.

That had definitely been a face. A person had been looking out at her.

Studying the picture she'd just taken, Lou saw nothing in the upstairs window. Nothing. But she'd seen a face in the window, however briefly, right?

Lou blinked, almost wondering if her eyes were playing tricks on her. Had she wanted something to happen so badly that her mind had fabricated a person? The itch between her shoulder blades returned.

But all questions of reality were moot as a great crash came spilling out of the mansion. The shattering of glass rang through the quiet street.

Finally, Lou had a legitimate reason to approach the mansion and sate her curiosity. She raced forward, darting right and left as she navigated the overgrown yard. The sagging front steps groaned as Lou vaulted up them. She knocked on the front door, but another crash inside had her rushing around the side of the house on the wraparound porch to her right. She stopped for a split second at a large window that looked in on an expansive kitchen.

There, on the tile floor, lay an older man. The blood pooling around him was dark red against the white floor tiles. A knife stuck out of his chest.

Lou caught movement to her right. A person raced through the trees and brush of the backyard. They wore a hood pulled up to cover their head.

"Hey! Stop!" Lou called toward them.

The person didn't even turn around as they fled the scene of the crime.

The urge to chase after them pushed her body forward, but her feet stayed put as she thought of the man lying on the floor in the kitchen. She couldn't leave him. He needed an ambulance immediately.

Knowing she wasn't going after the fleeing suspect, Lou did her best to memorize everything she could about them. She hadn't gotten close but could see the person wasn't much taller than her. They had a slight build and wore a black hooded sweatshirt and jeans.

Sure that the person was gone, Lou pulled out her phone as she raced around to the back of the house. The sliding glass door just off the kitchen was wide open. She jogged to the man's side. He was older—probably in his seventies, if she had to guess—with shaggy white hair and pale, sagging skin.

Lou didn't recognize him. In the six months she'd lived in Button, she'd never seen this man.

She knelt next to him, fingers trembling as she called 9-1-1. When the dispatcher answered, Lou explained where she was and what had happened.

"Is he still breathing?" the woman asked on the other end of the call.

Lou froze. She couldn't see any movement in his chest. His eyes were open, but vacant. She carefully felt his wrist, searching for a pulse.

There was none.

"I don't think so," Lou admitted, hanging her head.

"I'm sending help your way. Do you have a safe place to wait?" the woman asked.

Lou scanned the room. Now that the stabber was gone, she seemed to be alone. "Yes. I'll stay here."

She hung up the call and stood, wrapping her arms around her waist and hugging tight. Guilt consumed her; she'd stayed behind with the old man for nothing. She should've gone after the murderer.

Instead, Lou had allowed them to get away.

The itch between her shoulder blades wasn't gone, but it morphed from intense curiosity into an eerie chill. A creaking sound upstairs made the hair on Lou's arms stand on end. *Was* she safe here? The person she'd seen sneaking through the house had fled, right? She quieted her adrenaline-fueled heavy breathing and listened but heard nothing else. It must've just been the old house. Victorian-built houses like this one made a lot of noise.

Sweeping her eyes over the room, Lou detailed everything she could. If she hadn't gone after the killer, the least she could do was make it easier for Detective West and his officers to catch them.

The kitchen was enormous. And that measurement wasn't just in comparison with her small kitchen in the apartment above her bookshop. This place was twice as big as the substantial chef's kitchen back in her Manhattan condo. That kitchen along with the view of Central Park had sold her on the condo so many years ago and had made it a cinch for her to sell it earlier that year.

This kitchen held a large island in the center that housed a bulky Viking stove she might've pined for if it were in better condition. As it was, the steel was covered in grease, and many of the knobs were missing from the front. To her left, there was an eating nook in the kitchen. A dingy card table with two chairs sat in the small circular room with windows all around, overlooking the backyard. Well, what once must've been a backyard. Now, it was more like a forest with a dusty patch of earth between the patio and the trees crowding in. Someone had hastily set a bag of groceries on the countertop. It had toppled over and out had spilled jars of spaghetti sauce, boxes of macaroni and cheese, and a few cans of soup.

One of the jars of spaghetti sauce had fallen onto the floor in a display of shattered glass, and red tomato splattered like blood not ten feet away from the actual blood. One of the crashes she'd heard?

The groceries weren't the only things out of place, however. Stools that should've been tucked up to the kitchen island had toppled over on the floor as if there had been a struggle. But she didn't see signs of anything else broken that would answer for the second crash she'd heard.

She tried to piece everything together. Maybe this old man had just come back from grocery shopping, and he'd interrupted a burglar in the process of breaking and entering. In the struggle that ensued, they knocked over stools, and he'd dropped his groceries?

"Police!" a familiar voice called down the hallway, breaking Lou's line of thought.

"Easton, I'm in here." Lou paced, glancing down at the body once more.

It was in that moment that she noticed the handle on the knife sticking out of the old man's chest was the same gray handle as the set in the block on the counter. One of the larger slots was vacant, meaning the killer had used this man's own chef's knife against him.

Detective Easton West walked into the kitchen with a scowl already in place. A crime scene team flanked him, and footsteps creaked upstairs as other officers checked that the house was clear. EMTs raced forward, tending to the stabbed man. Lou felt certain he was gone but was glad she wasn't the one who had to make the call.

"Why am I not surprised you're here?" Easton asked, fixing her with a narrow-eyed glare.

Lou put up her hands as if she were in trouble. "I was just walking by when I heard a crash. I knocked on the door, but heard another crash. When I followed the porch around to the side of the house, I saw this man through the window and found the back door wide open." She peered over at the man with the knife stuck in his chest. The paramedics hadn't even attempted to start any life-saving procedures, so she'd been right about his state. "A person was running away through the backyard when I came in."

She described the person she'd seen while Easton jotted down the information and gave it to his officers with orders to search the surrounding area.

"I should've run after the person, but I thought I could help this man." Lou shook her head. "Turns out he was already gone."

Lou walked over to the open back door to show Easton the way the person had fled. The detective peered down at the dirt just past the poured-concrete patio. Lou noticed what had caught his eye right away. Shoe prints were clear in the dusty earth, documenting the bottom of a person's shoes. They followed the exact route the fleeing person had taken. Instead of the geometric lines or waves one might see on a normal sneaker, about a hundred stars covered the sole. Something about the pattern felt familiar to Lou. Her detail-oriented mind latched on to it in the way it often did when she recognized something. The only problem was, she couldn't place where she'd seen that pattern before.

Easton took a few pictures of the shoe prints before turning back to Lou. He held her gaze, his expression softening. "Hey, don't beat yourself up. I'm glad you didn't chase after the person. Even if you had caught up to them, what were you going to do? Tackle a murderer and wait until we got to wherever you had them pinned to the ground?"

The man had a point. Lou let go of the guilt as they reentered the kitchen crime scene.

"This man has been dead for at least an hour," called a paramedic over by the body.

Easton cocked an eyebrow in question.

"Rigor mortis is already setting in," the paramedic explained. He turned his attention to Lou. "And you said you arrived on the scene around what time? Five fifty-five?"

"Yes." Lou checked the time she'd taken the picture on her phone just to be sure.

"We'll have to wait for the medical examiner to know for sure," the paramedic said, "but I'd say this guy's been dead since closer to five o'clock this afternoon."

Five o'clock? Lou frowned. "But why would the stabber still be here almost an hour later?" She glanced around the kitchen.

Easton called over two officers documenting the scene nearby. "When you swept the house, were there any signs of robbery?"

The officers nodded.

"Upstairs, especially," one officer explained. "Stuff is strewn everywhere. There's a broken vase in the upstairs hallway. Someone was definitely searching for something."

The broken vase must've been the source of the other crash she'd heard. So the killer had been upstairs when they saw Lou, had knocked over a vase, had run downstairs to escape, and had bumped the spaghetti jar off the counter in the process.

"I thought it seemed like the victim had recently gotten

back from the grocery store and surprised a burglar," Lou said, voicing her suspicion from earlier.

But Easton shook his head.

"How can you be sure? Look, he was at the grocery store." She pointed at the overturned bag.

"Ron hasn't done his own grocery shopping in at least twenty years. He might have had groceries delivered, but he hasn't left this house." He checked the plain paper grocery bag for a receipt but came up empty handed. "Robbery, maybe, but I wouldn't be surprised if everything finally caught up to him after all these years." Easton's eyes narrowed for a split second as if he was doing the math in his head.

Lou was about to ask what Easton meant by that comment when the medical examiner entered the room, stealing away the detective's attention.

But Lou's focus wasn't so easily diverted. Now she had more questions than ever. Who had Ron been? Why hadn't he left his house for twenty years? And what was Easton so sure had finally caught up to him?

CHAPTER 3

I t felt wrong for Lou to continue on to Willow's house for dinner after Easton let her leave the crime scene. Keeping her original plans for dinner felt like it somehow erased the fact that she'd just stumbled upon a dead body. But she definitely didn't want to go home and spend the evening alone, even more so now.

The chilling reality that Ben's birthday—already a tough day to get through—had only gotten worse now that it shared the death of a local man pulled at the remaining threads of Lou's happiness.

Lou ambled the rest of the way to her friend's little green farmhouse across the street from the mansion. Easton's neat gray house next door was the opposite to Willow's in almost every way. While Willow's porch was crowded with plants and knickknacks, Easton's was immaculate and sparse. The only decoration on his porch was a carved bear holding a welcome sign.

Their houses perfectly encompassed their opposite personalities, reflected by the constant butting of heads that happened between them. Though Lou had recently confirmed a longtime

23

suspicion that Easton didn't hate Willow as much as he pretended to. In fact, he sounded a whole lot like he was in love with her. Lou shook the distracting thoughts from her mind and jogged up to Willow's front door. She didn't knock, just let herself in, calling out a hello as she closed the door behind her.

The two lifelong best friends had exchanged keys to show that either was welcome at the other's home anytime, so Lou never technically needed to knock, but especially not when Willow was expecting her, late as she was.

Hearing no response to her greeting, Lou checked the kitchen and living room. Finding them empty, Lou knew where to go next: out back in the barn. She headed out through the sliding glass door to Willow's porch. From there, a lush lawn, beds of flowers, and many potted plants made up Willow's garden. Beyond that was a small barn with two paddocks and behind that, a large, sandy arena and a round pen.

The sounds of stamping hooves and a snorting horse were carried from the barn on the summer evening wind. Standing sentry at the entrance to the barn was a gray pygmy goat.

"Steven." Lou inclined her head and saluted the goat.

Normally, Steve would've been wearing a pair of his adorable signature pajamas—because in Willow's words, "Why not?"—but it was summer, and the temperatures were creeping up into the eighties, which was hot for the Pacific Northwest.

Lou slipped past the goat, who followed behind her with small clomping hooves, and walked toward the crossties where Willow normally groomed OC, her large chestnut gelding. OC was short for Of Course, part of the theme song for one of Willow's favorite old-timey shows, *Mr. Ed*. The crossties were empty, but Lou heard noises in the stall to her right. She peered through the metal bars that kept the horse from sticking his long neck out and grabbing at things that weren't supposed to be nibbled on.

Inside, Willow was clapping alfalfa dust off her gloved hands. OC munched happily on his dinner.

"Hey," Lou said with a smile.

"Hay," Willow said in return, laughing as she plucked a handful of hay from OC's mane. She glanced up at Lou and froze. "Whoa, what happened?" Willow raced over to her. "You're pale. Are you feeling okay?"

"You know that house I was asking you about earlier?" Lou scratched at the back of her neck, hoping to relieve the icy feeling that spread as she thought about the scene she'd just left.

Willow nodded warily.

"When I was on my way here, I saw someone in the window, and then there was a crash."

Willow pulled OC's stall door closed, but not until after the goat slipped inside to be with his buddy. "Please tell me you didn't go inside. That sounds like the beginning of a horror movie."

Lou cringed. "I did, and it kind of was. Someone lives there —well, they did. I found him with a knife stabbed into his chest." Lou shook her head when Willow shot her a hopeful glance. "He was already dead when I arrived. There was a person running away when I got there. They were wearing a dark hood, so I couldn't see their face."

"So, the person sneaking around was the one who stabbed him?" Willow asked, proving she wasn't completely oblivious to details.

"That's what I'm thinking," Lou said, "but Easton will figure it out, I'm sure. He said it could be a robbery."

"A robbery?" Willow shivered. "That's creepy, especially since it happened across the street."

"You have a pretty good security system, I'd say." Lou arched her eyebrow.

"Steve?" Willow asked, peering into the stall to find the goat.

Lou laughed. "No, living next to a detective."

"Oh, yeah ..." Willow didn't seem convinced as her gaze wandered off into the distance. Her eyes narrowed as she scowled past Lou, through the opening at the other end of the barn. "Lou ... when you said a dark hood, did you mean like that?" Willow pointed, her finger shaking slightly.

Past her arena and round pen, there was a line of trees before the next piece of property. About two hundred feet away, movement in the tree line made Lou's breath catch in her throat. A person with a black hood pulled up to cover their head snuck along the fence line of Willow's property.

Lou flattened herself against the wall. Willow followed her lead. Hoping the hooded stabber hadn't seen them, Lou pulled out her phone and called Easton.

"Hey, I'm—" he answered, but Lou cut him off.

"I think the person I saw at the scene of the crime is creeping along the tree line on the western end of Willow's property," Lou whispered into her phone even though she was sure the sneaking person was too far away to hear her.

"On my way. Stay inside." He barked out the order and then hung up.

Moments later, his car pulled up to the edge of the property. Easton and a uniformed officer raced out of the cruiser, guns drawn. Lou and Willow held their breath as Easton and the officer disappeared into the small grouping of trees.

They walked out a moment later, pushing a person in a black hood into the back of the cruiser. Lou got a text on her phone that said,

Good work. I think this is our suspect. Taking them in for questioning.

Lou's heartbeat slowed. She showed Willow the text from Easton, and they exhaled in relief.

"Well, I guess that solves it." An odd mix of feelings filled Lou. She was sad for the man who'd been killed but glad the murderer was off the streets.

Willow seemed to sense her friend's unease. "Let's head inside," she said. "Dinner is all ready. I just need to toss in the dressing and warm up the chicken."

Lou's stomach grumbled. She hadn't realized how hungry she was until then. She followed Willow inside. They were just walking into the kitchen when her phone rang. It was Joe, Ben's brother.

Wiggling her phone in the air, Lou asked, "You mind if I talk to Joey real quick?"

Willow shook her head and started pulling things out of the fridge.

Ever since Ben had passed, his older brother had been good about checking on Lou to make sure she was doing okay, especially around holidays or days that were important for her and Ben. He'd called on their anniversary, so it was no surprise he was calling today. Lou had meant to call him this time, but the day had gotten away from her with her discovery of the dead body and all. She loved her brother-in-law, but sometimes he was a little too much like Ben for comfort. They had the same voice, the same booming laugh, even the same dark beard.

"Hey, Sis," Joe said when Lou answered, a tenderness in his voice that made Lou sure he was tilting his head to one side. "How ya doing?"

"I'm good, Joey." Lou tried to make her voice sound normal. She knew Joe was already worried about her, and telling him she'd just stumbled upon a stabbing victim wouldn't help. "How are you and the family?" Between the tightness in her tone and the tremors as she spoke, she knew she failed.

But Joe must've attributed her unsteadiness to the date instead of anything more sinister because he said, "Hanging in there. Thinking of Ben a lot today." Joe's voice caught as he uttered his brother's name. "Speaking of the fam, I was going to ask what you thought about having some visitors."

Lou inhaled. "Oh, that would be wonderful." She wet her lips as she thought. "I mean, I only have the one guest room, but if the girls don't mind air mattresses, we can set them up in the living room. There are a couple of cute local hotels, too, if you would rather have a little more space. My new place is a little smaller than New York, which is saying something." She laughed, but was acutely aware of how fake it sounded.

As much as she loved her family, she wasn't sure if she was ready to have company right now.

"Actually," Joe said, stopping her worries for a moment, "it would just be the girls. Em got invited to speak at a conference up in Canada, kind of last minute. She wasn't going to take it, at first, because it's ... well, it starts on Wednesday and goes through Sunday, the twenty-fourth."

Lou swallowed the ball of emotion that built in her throat. The twenty-fourth of July was the anniversary of Ben's death.

"We didn't want to leave the girls alone, but they insisted we go," Joe explained.

Lou nodded along. Her nieces were sixteen and seventeen, and more than capable of taking care of themselves for a week or so, but Lou knew it had more to do with Joe and Emily not wanting to leave them alone during that specific anniversary.

"Well, the girls had a fantastic idea," Joe continued. "Since it's summer, they thought they could come spend a week or two with you while we're away. Keep you company and all."

Lou's heart melted. "I would love that. As much as I would love to see you and Emily, it would be really fun to have it be just me and the girls. Yes, anytime."

Willow's eyes lit up. She listened to Lou's end of the conversation as she and Joe worked out the rest of the details about the visit.

"And you've warned them about my new town?" Lou asked. "It's not as glamorous as New York City."

Joe scoffed, "You've seen where we live. They're used to small-town life."

Lou supposed that was true. The other part of the Henry family lived in small-town Montana. "Okay, well, it's all set. Just send me their flight information when you have it, and I'll be there to pick them up from the airport." She paused. "One more thing, Joey."

"Yeah?" he asked.

Lou chewed on her lip. "There was a man murdered in town today." She stopped there, not feeling like it was necessary to go into the details of how she was the one who found him. "It sounds like the police caught the person responsible, but I just want to make sure you're okay with sending the girls when that's so fresh."

Joe laughed. "Sorry. I'm not laughing about the murder. That's awful. It's just that we sent them to New York, didn't we? I think they'll be okay. They're smart, and I trust you to keep them safe."

"Okay." She felt the same but had wanted Joe and Emily to have all the information. "I'll look forward to seeing them."

She hung up the call. Willow let out an excited squeal. "We get the girls? For how long?"

"Sounds like two whole weeks," she said.

But while the smile on Lou's face wasn't forced, the emotions rushing through her were a lot more complicated. Being the first anniversary of Ben's death, she wasn't sure how it would hit her, how she would react. She'd expected to work through the feelings on her own, maybe with help from Willow, if she needed. The girls were loud bundles of love and hugs. And even though she knew they would share in her sadness, she worried that she'd have to pretend to be happier than she was to keep her guests comfortable.

Willow studied Lou for a moment before saying, "Okay, honest three."

It was a saying they'd come up with to check in with one another over the years, cutting right to the three most prevalent emotions they were feeling at any given moment. Willow had obviously caught that Lou wasn't being completely honest about her feelings.

Lou inhaled. With a slow exhale, she said, "Missing him, scared, apprehensive."

Willow frowned. "Scared?"

Lou nodded. "Mostly about the whole finding-a-man-stabbed-to-death thing." She thought for a moment. "But a little scared about having to live the rest of my life as a series of anniversaries that used to be joyful and are now hard, emotional days I have to get through. Birthdays and anniversaries used to be the brief hints of sparkle throughout the calendar, and now they're dark spots that I have to dread and survive. I really thought I would handle this better, honestly."

Because Ben's death had been so sudden, Lou had tried to focus on the wonderful life they'd had together, instead of wallowing in self-pity about what she was missing. But on days like today, it was harder to hold on to that optimistic attitude.

"Right." Willow gave her friend a small smile. "How could we make them good again? What if we do something super fun each year on Ben's birthday?"

Lou liked that idea. "Yeah, let's think about it."

Willow held her glass up to Lou's, sealing the promise with a clink. With that, a little piece of fear chipped away from Lou's heart. Willow's idea gave her something positive to think about in relation to Ben's birthday. And wasn't that the trick? Looking on the positive side of things always made Lou feel better.

For example, Lou may have stumbled onto a murder, but at least the police had caught the killer. Justice had been served. It didn't answer her questions about the identity of the dead man. Knowing that his name had been Ron wouldn't help her search, nor did she want to bug Easton when he had his hands full with the murderer.

It seemed she would have to wait a little longer for answers, but she was confident she would get them. She always did.

CHAPTER 4

The next morning, Lou opened the bookshop to only two of her three regulars. George was nowhere to be found, nor did she answer when Lou texted to see if she was okay, which was unusual. The two regulars who had shown were oddly quiet and restless for the first few minutes, awkwardly glancing in Lou's direction. Silas kept peering at her over the top of his newspaper. Forrest had cleared his throat about thirteen times before Lou finally had too much.

"Okay, what's up with you two?" she asked, placing a hand on her hip. "And where's George?"

Forrest cleared his throat again, and Silas ducked behind his newspaper.

But a moment later, Silas grumbled something about being the only one who knew how to handle this and then in a louder voice said, "We heard you had a run-in at the mansion on Thread Lane last night."

Lou folded her arms in front of her. "Oh, *now* we're willing to discuss the mansion? *Now* you're willing to admit that it exists?"

"Sorry, Lou. We really thought it was for the best," Forrest added. "We've been keeping that place at the back of our collective minds for so many years now, it just didn't seem like the right time to bring it up."

Lou inclined her head. "Don't worry about it. I'm not sure knowing anything more than I did would've helped the situation. The man I found had already been dead for an hour when I got there, and Easton caught the killer."

"So what happened?" Silas asked. "Who'd Easton arrest?"

"Oh, no you don't." Lou wagged a finger at them. "You have some explaining to do before I tell you anything."

The men bobbed their heads in agreement, resigned to their fate.

"Fair enough," Forrest said. "What do you want to know?"

"Easton said something about how, Ron, the guy who lived there never left the house. Why?" She leaned her elbows on the counter, settling in for what she assumed would be an involved tale.

Forrest puffed out his cheeks in an exhale. "Well ... we might as well tell you the entire story. It's all wrapped up together. What has it been, now?" Forrest squinted one eye as he studied the ceiling.

"Twenty years tomorrow," Silas said, his tone flat.

"That sounds about right." Forrest nodded somberly. "Have you been to Tinsdale?" Forrest asked.

"Yes," Lou said tentatively.

"So you've seen the steel mill?" Silas asked.

"Sure. The one that's no longer in business?" she asked.

"Ronald Rossback, the man you found last night, was the owner of that steel mill," Forrest explained.

Lou leaned forward, interest piqued.

"His father owned it before that," Silas jumped in. "And his grandfather before that. But Ronald wasn't like the rest of his family. He was a lazy, worthless human who chose profits and his own comfort over the security and safety of his workers." Silas crumpled his face into a scowl, and Lou was sure he would've spat on the ground if he'd been outside.

Forrest held up a hand. "There were *some* extenuating circumstances. When Ron took over that mill close to forty years ago, the steel trade had already begun moving overseas. America-made steel was becoming less and less sought after, in favor of the cheaper stuff companies could get shipped in. He saw the writing on the wall and knew enough about business to see that his family's mill wouldn't last much into the new century."

"Then he should've closed it down, let the workers find different jobs," Silas barked as if Forrest were Ronald.

"He should've," Forrest agreed.

"But he didn't?" Lou guessed. "What did he do instead?" Her forehead wrinkled.

"He didn't take care of the place," Silas said. "The accident was completely avoidable."

Lou flinched at the word "accident."

Forrest scoffed, "Accident isn't the word for what happened. Ronald knew the business wouldn't be profitable for long, so he siphoned as much money as he could out of it. He only did basic maintenance on the machines so he could pass the state inspections, but he cut corners everywhere else and didn't invest in new technology when it clearly would've made working conditions safer."

"The workers complained to him constantly," Silas said. "But Ron never listened to their very valid concerns about the state of the equipment they worked with every day." Silas snorted in disgust. "Some quit because of the conditions, but most couldn't afford to leave."

Dread built in Lou the more they described the setup.

"And there was an accident?" she asked, her voice small.

Forrest nodded gravely.

"One of the blast furnaces exploded. It hadn't been maintained well, and it developed a crack that let in too much oxygen. Five people died. Dozens more were injured," Silas explained.

Forrest stroked Anne Mice's back, the stiffness in the set of his shoulders loosening a little. "They gave Ronald an opportunity to fix the machines, but between the fines and the lawsuits that poured in, he closed the mill, leaving a thousand people out of work overnight."

"And basically shut down the entire city of Tinsdale, from what I've heard." Lou remembered driving into the city with Willow. The place was a ghost town.

"Many people had to stay because of the housing bubble that was created locally when so many people tried to sell at once," Forrest explained.

"It's why Ronald stayed in that stupid mansion of his," Silas grumbled. "At first, he couldn't sell. Then he became somewhat of a recluse and didn't want to leave."

Lou had been wondering about that. Why else would someone stick around where they'd created so much heartbreak, where everyone hated them?

"And what does this whole thing have to do with George?" Lou asked. A growing feeling of dread for her young friend had been building through the entire conversation.

Silas looked down at his hands.

"Her father was one of the workers who died." Forrest's head dropped forward as if he were standing by a friend's grave.

Poor George. The news hit Lou even harder as she remembered the moment George had first learned of Lou's widow status. George had mentioned that you never knew what pain people were hiding when everything seemed okay. Lou hadn't even thought to ask if the young woman was hiding the same pain.

"So that's why her grandparents raised her?" Lou asked.

Silas nodded. "George and her father, Lewis, were already living with his parents. George's momma passed away from a complication during childbirth. Lewis knew he wouldn't be able to take care of George alone, so he moved them in with his parents. After he passed, those two were all George had in this world."

Lou's heart ached as she listened to the details of baby George's life. If this had all happened twenty years ago, George couldn't have been more than a couple of years old when her father passed.

"I'm so sorry for bringing it up around her yesterday." Lou groaned, placing a hand over her heart.

Forrest shook his head. "Don't beat yourself up, Lou. That girl was raised by two people who loved her more than the world itself—not to mention the support she always had from the entire town. Lewis and Joy were part of this town's core."

Lou discerned that this was likely another reason George hadn't ever moved away from her small hometown. Not only was she skilled at helping the technologically insecure people of Button, but they were her family.

"So you think someone came and killed Ron to get revenge for the steel mill accident?" Lou asked.

Silas puffed out his chest. "Revenge makes the most sense to me."

"Easton seemed to think it was a robbery when he was at the scene yesterday," Lou said.

"Maybe at first, but if he didn't realize the proximity of the twentieth anniversary yesterday, he has by now," Forrest said.

That was when Lou realized she might have experienced the very moment the detective had put it all together. When

Easton had narrowed his eyes yesterday and appeared to be doing math in his head, had he been counting the years since the accident?

"He seemed pretty sure that the person they apprehended last night was the suspect in Ron's murder." Lou shrugged.

"Easton didn't give you a name?" Forrest asked.

"No," Lou admitted, "but in order for him to say that so definitively, I think it must have been a person connected to one of the five who died."

Silas shook his head. "I wouldn't be so quick to make that assumption. Sure, the families who lost a loved one suffered the most, but many of those who were hurt could never rejoin the workforce because of their injuries. And even the people who lost their jobs could've grown bitter over all these years. I knew many people who lost their homes, drained their savings; everything became a struggle as a result of the closure. Seeing that snake living in that big house, like nothing could touch him, it would've driven me mad."

"Though, seeing the house fall into disrepair as it has brings me a little satisfaction, I have to say," Forrest added.

A customer entered the bookshop. She was a local Lou had seen around town—at the grocery store and in line at the coffee shop—and her gaze rested on Lou too long for her to be there for only books. She wanted information.

"Good morning," Lou said. "Can I help you find anything?"

"Oh, I'm just here to browse. Good for you, staying open after everything you went through yesterday." The woman placed a hand over her heart.

Subtle segue, Lou thought with an inward chuckle.

She was about to thank the woman for her concern when Silas jumped in and said, "Oh, get off it, Linda. We all know you came in here to gossip. You can stop the act. Lou doesn't know who was arrested."

Linda gasped and wore an offended expression. Lou noticed she didn't deny the accusation, though. She bustled off into the new-releases section of the store, shooting an angry glare over her shoulder at Silas as she went past.

Silence engulfed the bookshop, Linda's entrance acting as a metaphorical pause button on the conversation. Silas and Forrest focused on the cats and turned back to their reading as if their earlier conversation hadn't ever occurred.

Minutes later, Linda reappeared at the checkout counter, a book clutched in her hands. She smiled at Lou and pushed the book forward. "I've been meaning to pick this up for a while now. I'm so glad my schedule allowed for me to come get it today," Linda said.

Lou couldn't help but notice how the woman spoke loudly enough for Silas to hear, or how obviously she was trying to justify her visit so she wouldn't be branded a gossip. But Lou also knew that the particular book Linda was purchasing was a brand new release and had just gone out on the shelves a few days ago. So there was no way she'd been meaning to pick it up for a while unless she was studying the soon-to-be-released lists from the publishing houses. But while Lou highly doubted that was the case, she also didn't want to push anything with Linda. The woman was spending money in her store, under false pretenses or not.

"Thanks for coming in," Lou said as she handed over the book in a bag once Linda had paid.

The conversation about Ronald and the steel mill never picked back up. Many more "Lindas" came through that day. It almost became repetitive, to the point that by the end of the day, Lou didn't look up when the door opened; it was probably just one more local on the search for gossip.

"Special delivery," Willow said, stopping in front of Lou.

Lou glanced up as her best friend flourished her arms

toward the white Button School District utility truck parked in front of the bookstore. Lou wondered why Willow was driving a school vehicle during her summer break. She got her answer as she followed Willow outside and saw two flowering dogwood trees in the truck's bed.

Their vibrant pink flowers almost took Lou's breath away. They were so gorgeous. Willow had been dropping off trees for Lou to use outside the shop since she'd moved there, citing their need for a different location or time to heal from being around the high schoolers. Lou's frown remained as she thought through what she knew about dogwoods. They usually flowered in spring, not summer.

Willow read her friend's expression exactly. "Don't even ask," she said, but then added, "A local brought these in during the spring because they weren't blooming. The kids and I worked on them, repotting, fertilizing, everything we could think of, but we couldn't get them to bloom. Now that school's out, the custodian called me and told me they'd finally opened up. So I figured you could enjoy them."

They spent a few minutes situating the trees in front of the shop windows and dousing them with a good drink of water. Excess water drained out of the bottom of the planters and trickled down the warm sidewalk.

"Oh, I forgot. I have a new gardening book for you inside." Lou waved a hand for Willow to follow her.

Willow's face broke into a huge grin, and she tugged the gardening gloves off her hands. She trailed behind Lou, eagerness evident in her quick steps. Lou beamed as she watched her best friend peruse the new book. Willow's eyes lit up, and she showed off a few of the features of the pages she was excited about.

By the time they walked back outside, they were both smiling, Willow clutching the large gardening tome as if it were a treasure. But Lou's smile dropped into a frown. Her attention caught on the sidewalk in front of the shop. The water from the trees had created little rivers of water heading for the storm drains in the road. Wet footprints marked up the concrete in front of the bookstore. The prints were all from the same shoes and made a pattern as if someone had been pacing in front of the shop.

The most chilling thing, however, was that the print was comprised of hundreds of tiny stars, just like Lou and Easton had seen in the dirt behind the mansion where the suspect had fled the scene yesterday. Posture rigid, Lou pulled out her phone and snapped a couple of pictures.

"What's the problem?" Willow asked.

"Those are the same prints I saw at the scene of the murder last night." Lou shivered and wondered how likely it was for that pattern to show up so close to her so soon after a murder. She had a bad feeling that it wasn't a coincidence.

CHAPTER 5

If Lou had been on her own when she'd discovered the wet footprints, she might've thought about it, done some research, and then consulted Easton in the morning if she was still feeling worried.

But Lou wasn't alone.

Willow gasped, checking over her shoulder as if a killer might be hiding there. Then she used the large gardening book as a plow to shove Lou back inside the bookshop.

"Lock the door. I'm calling Easton right now." Willow plastered herself to the window and held the phone to her ear as she peered up and down the quiet street.

"Willow, I'm fine," Lou said, trying to remain calm. "More than one person probably has those shoes. I overreacted when I said that—"

But Lou couldn't finish because Willow already had Easton on the phone. "Hey, come to the bookstore now. Lou's in danger." She hung up.

"Willow!" Lou held a hand out to stop her friend. "You can't say something like that. The poor guy is going to—"

She broke off as Easton skidded to a halt in front of the

bookshop. He saw them inside and ran to the front door. But he hadn't expected it to be locked, so he pushed forward and smacked his forehead into the door.

Willow's hand flew to cover her mouth as a surprised groan leaked out of her. Lou just cringed, feeling awful that she'd created this situation by being overly dramatic about the shoe prints.

Jogging over to the door, Lou carefully unlocked it, creasing her face into an apology. She dragged the door open and stepped aside as Easton took a moment to enter.

"Willow," Easton said slowly, like her name was a warning. His eyes were focused on the ground as if he was worried his angry glare might physically burn her. When he finally looked up, he calmly said, "You made it sound like Lou was currently getting murdered. I was in line to get ice cream." He gestured animatedly to the shop next door.

"Sorry." Willow wrinkled her nose, then pointed out toward the sidewalk. "But the killer's shoe prints were out in front of the bookshop. They were in a pacing pattern, like they were waiting to get inside, like they were trying to figure out their next move."

Easton pinched the bridge of his nose as Willow spoke, but at her last statement, Easton's worried gaze flicked around the room and then out the window.

Lou frowned in confusion. "You caught the person last night, though, right?" she asked in a shaky voice.

Easton shifted his weight. "What?" His cheeks reddened.

"We watched you catch the killer last night, cutting behind Willow's property. If you caught them, why'd you come running so quickly?" Lou motioned to outside the window. "And just then, it seemed like you thought I might actually be in grave danger."

Easton held up his hands in a gesture of calm, but it did

nothing to soothe Lou. In fact, the gesture only made her whole body pulse with fear and anxiety.

"What happened?" she asked.

Glancing over his shoulder, Easton said, "The person we caught sneaking around Willow's last night wasn't the killer."

Lou's stomach dropped. The sense of safety she'd felt vanished. Lou hadn't realized how much thinking they had apprehended the killer had been helping her mood until it was proven otherwise. "How can that be? You seemed so sure it was them last night."

"Do you have any customers right now?" Easton asked.

"No. It's just us," Lou said.

Easton motioned over to the table to sit. Lou followed, along with Willow.

"I think you deserve to know what happened twenty years ago." He watched her somberly.

Lou folded her hands in her lap. "I heard the whole story. The accident. The people who died. I figured the person you caught last night was someone who lost a loved one in that accident, right?"

Willow sputtered out a string of unintelligible words in surprise. She composed herself enough to say, "Wait, what? I've heard none of this."

"I'll tell you the details later," Lou said with a wave of her hand, "but basically Ronald used to own the steel mill in Tinsdale. He didn't maintain the machines, and there was an accident that killed five people and injured many more. The twenty-year anniversary of that accident is tomorrow," Lou said, shooting her friend a look that told her that was all she was getting of the story.

Easton pulled in a long breath before he began his explanation. "You're right, Lou. The anniversary being tomorrow makes it a distinct possibility revenge motivated Ronald's murder. And at first, I thought it was going to be that easy because the person sneaking by Willow's house was connected, but ..." He shook his head.

"The person we saw creeping around my property last night was connected to the steel mill accident? That can't be a coincidence!" Willow said, voicing Lou's concerns in a much louder, emotional way than Lou ever would.

Easton flinched. "I'm sorry, it is. The person has an airtight alibi."

"Then why were they sneaking through the woods?" Lou crossed her arms.

Easton checked out the window as if someone might read his lips. "Look, let's just say that the person was at a *meeting* until six fifteen. Many people saw her. The *meeting*, as well as the upcoming anniversary, upset her enough that she was crying. She was just walking home, taking the shortcut behind Willow's property up to her house and didn't want anyone to see that she was upset. That's why she had the hood of her jacket raised."

"A meeting?" Lou asked, focusing on the emphasis Easton had put on the word each time. Her eyes widened. "Ah," she said as it clicked. A meeting, like for alcohol or drug dependence. Sympathy for the woman and her difficulties with substance abuse rose above Lou's irritation.

Easton nodded. "The person we detained last night couldn't have been the one to stab Ron at five o'clock."

Willow sighed.

"Her shoes didn't match the star prints we found at the scene either," Easton explained. "I brought her in for questioning anyway because I thought she might've changed shoes, but once her alibi was sound, I knew it wasn't her."

Lou had to agree with Easton. It seemed to make sense.

"Okay, so these could've been made by the actual killer,

then," Lou said, pulling up the pictures she'd taken on her phone. The prints had most likely dried up in the summer evening sunshine at that point, so they would have to rely on the pictures.

Easton leaned forward to look. "That definitely resembles the print we found out back behind Ron's house."

Lou flipped to the next shot, which showed the erratic pattern of the prints.

"Maybe they dropped something and had to come back for it," Easton said.

"Multiple times?" Willow turned to him in an exasperated, *do something about it* way.

"I researched the shoes," Easton said. "They're a very popular brand. It won't be easy to find the culprit based on their shoe brand." Easton cut the air with his palm in a definitive way that made Lou sure that arguing wouldn't help.

Willow didn't get that message. "In movies, the footprint *always* helps find the killer." She stood and paced around the round table next to the checkout counter in the bookstore.

Easton's nostrils flared. "Again, it's not that easy. How many times do I have to remind you that my job is not like the movies, Willow? This is real life. Life and death."

Willow stopped pacing. "I know it's life and death. It's the life of my best friend, and I can't do life without her. I don't think you get how important she is to me."

Lou sent a soft smile toward her friend. As much as she loved Willow for sticking up for her, Lou was pretty sure Easton understood how much Lou meant to Willow. In fact, he'd tried to be as nice and helpful to Lou as he could since she'd moved there, with the sole purpose of gaining favor with Willow.

Seeing the detective needed assistance with her fiery best friend, Lou stood.

"Willow, he's right. I'm sorry I freaked you out. It was

wrong of me to say such an alarming thing and not expect you to react." She held her hands out and fanned them slowly, like Willow did sometimes when OC was acting up and she wanted him to calm down. "What I should've done was take the pictures and find the brand on the internet to see what kind of popularity we were looking at. Once I saw that they're a fairly popular shoe, I would've realized it was probably not the person I saw at the mansion."

"Right," Easton agreed. "The safest thing that Lou and you can do is to stay as far away from this investigation as possible. This case carries a lot of history with it, and it's safer for everyone if you two stay out of things."

He was right, of course. Between Ben's birthday and the impending first anniversary of his death, she was having a tough time emotionally and mentally already. There was also the reality that she would be hosting her nieces soon. She didn't need to add anything more to her plate.

"I have no reason to get involved," Lou said.

Easton turned toward Willow. "Okay?"

Willow didn't look up, still fuming as she studied the floor.

"But what if they saw me? The actual killer, that is." Lou's stomach clenched tight with a concern she hadn't realized until now. "My nieces are coming to visit on Monday. Should I tell them not to come?"

"I think you'll be fine. But I know you'll have to do what you feel comfortable with." Easton must've felt bad for having to put Lou back into a state of worry. He rubbed at his wrist. "I've checked with the grocery store, and they're looking into anyone who might've delivered groceries to Ron. I'm also investigating the other people connected to the accident. Don't worry. We'll find them." With a wave, he was gone.

Lou made her way over to Willow. "Hey," she said softly, "it's really okay. I'm fine."

Willow glanced up, but her attention focused behind Lou toward the door. Shoulders relaxing, Willow's amiable smile returned. "Oh, I know. I realized about halfway through that interaction that I was wrong, but I didn't want to have to admit that in front of Easton, so I just pretended to be mad still."

Lou shook her head. "The two of you are ..." She couldn't finish that sentence without giving away what she knew about Easton's feelings about Willow.

Because he was just as stubborn as Willow was. He was doing the same thing. It was why he was continuing the antagonistic neighborly relationship of theirs. He'd originally started that way because he'd genuinely hated James, Willow's cheating ex-fiancé. But once Willow and James broke up, Easton had admitted that he wasn't sure how to change the dynamic between them. He was stuck with the first decision he'd made, just like Willow, with the argument they'd just had.

Well, the two of them deserve one another, Lou realized with an inward chuckle.

"Do you need to get that truck back to the high school?" Lou asked, motioning outside.

Willow scoffed, "Nah, it's fine. What we need to do is start a list of suspects." She pulled a blank piece of paper from the printer and situated herself behind the computer.

As much as Lou agreed with Easton that she didn't need to get involved, it seemed smart to at least make a list of the people she should be wary of. That way, she would know who to steer clear of, especially once her nieces were in town. She took charge of the note-taking as Willow searched for information online about the accident.

Luckily, unlike the mansion, there was plenty of news surrounding the steel mill accident in Tinsdale. There had been five victims:

- Lewis Greenwood, twenty-seven, survived by his daughter, George, and his parents, Henry and Lois.
- David Foreman, thirty, survived by his son, Aiden, and his wife, Heather.
- Jessie Coops, twenty-three, wasn't married and didn't have any children. His parents and sisters lived on the East Coast.
- Chance Trimble, fifty, was also without a partner or children. His parents had died years earlier.
- James Meredith, twenty-two, was survived by his wife, Scarlett.

"The person sneaking at the edge of my property must've been Scarlett Meredith," Willow said definitively.

"How do you know?" Lou's eyes darted up to Willow, the list in front of her momentarily forgotten.

Willow shrugged. "Scarlett works at the high school with me, though she teaches math. Whenever we go out to celebrate as a staff, she's really open about her status as a recovering alcoholic. Plus, she lives in the neighborhood up to the north from my house, so it would make sense that she would cut through that pathway behind my property."

"So Scarlett has an airtight alibi," Lou said. Then, as if spurred on by Scarlett's status, Lou began striking out the less-likely suspects. "George is also out." She drew a line through their friend's name.

Willow pointed to the list. "And I would say Jessie and Chance aren't going to lead to suspects since Chance didn't have any surviving family and Jessie's is all on the East Coast."

Lou agreed, striking out those names. And while Lou knew she couldn't completely rule them out, it seemed much less likely that it was connected to one of them. Which left Aiden and Heather Foreman.

Willow found records online that showed they both lived in Silver Lake, just south of Button. Aiden was in his early twenties, and had little more than a picture or two on social media and a few mentions from his time at Silver Lake High. Heather, in her fifties now, was a prominent surgeon at the big county hospital in Kirk.

An hour into their research, Lou and Willow looked at each other and sighed.

"Okay, so if we see either Aiden or Heather Foreman, we know to call Easton." Lou sat back, feeling helpless.

"Which he probably already knows since he said he was investigating people connected to the accident." Willow's shoulders slumped forward. "I think he was right. It doesn't seem like we need to get involved."

"Then let's not," Lou said. "Especially if the killer possibly knows who I am and where I live. I don't want to give them any other reasons to come after me." The back of Lou's neck went cold at the thought.

CHAPTER 6

Whiskers and Words was hopping the next morning. Lou wasn't sure if the influx of customers was due to continued interest surrounding the murder, and her involvement in finding the body, or if this was what normal summer tourism numbers were like.

Either way, Lou was happy. Happy and busy. Even the used-book section was rather picked over by the end of her first hour open. Lou's grin only widened as she recognized a customer walking in who had a special order waiting for her on the shelf. Forgetting her name, Lou consulted the order sheet sticking out of the book to remind herself. She knew how much the locals liked that small-town feeling of being on a first-name basis everywhere they went.

"Hi, Faith," Lou greeted her. "You just grabbing your order or doing some shopping?"

Faith squinted an eye and said, "I think I'll look around a little, if you don't mind."

"Of course." Lou grabbed Faith's special order from the shelf behind her and got it ready for whenever she was done shopping. She was just looking up from Faith's book about antique collectables when a woman she'd never seen before stomped over to the counter.

"How can I help you?" Lou asked a woman with graying curly brown hair pulled back into a clip.

"I was going to shop for a book, but I can't even breathe in this place." The woman held a used tissue to her nose and blew.

Lou winced. "I'm so sorry. There are warning signs on the front door, though. Are you allergic to cats?"

The woman pushed back her shoulders. "Severely. I should sue you for putting my life in danger by having these cats in your shop."

"It's clearly marked on the door." Lou pointed in case the woman had any doubt. "I have all the correct permits. I'm so sorry you're allergic. You can either travel to the next town over where they have a bookshop, or you can call, and I will mail you the order so you don't have to set foot inside the shop."

The woman scoffed, unhappy with that answer. She blew her nose again. "Well, I never ..." She mumbled something to herself just as Faith came up and stood behind her in line.

"I'm sorry, but would you mind stepping aside? I have other customers to assist," Lou said, steeling her tone. She may not have picked up much of a New York accent in her time living in the Big Apple, but she had latched on to their blunt way of speaking, and she wasn't afraid of a confrontation. She motioned for Faith to step forward.

"This is preposterous! It's just disgusting," the woman spluttered as Faith stepped around her.

"Nothing else?" Lou asked Faith, trying to tune out the angry customer. Maybe if she stopped responding to the woman's outbursts, she would leave.

Faith nervously regarded the fuming woman, who paced and blew her nose behind Faith. "Just that one," Faith said, gesturing to the book she'd had Lou order in. "There's another

I'm searching for, but I couldn't find it in the nonfiction section. I was hoping you could check in your computer to see if you could order it."

"So you'll help her, but not me," the upset woman screeched as she paced behind Faith.

"You haven't asked for any help," Lou pointed out. "Did you have a question, or do you just want to complain at me?" Lou waited for the woman to answer. When she didn't, Lou returned to Faith's request. "Let's see." Lou squinted at the computer screen, typing in the title of another book about antiques. "I'm afraid it's not something I can order. It seems to be out of print, which means you'll need to ask at some of the local used and rare book dealers."

Luckily, Lou knew of one in Silver Lake. She gave Faith Lance Swatek's information and hoped he could locate the book for her.

"You could also try talking to Smitty," Lou recommended. "The owner of the antique shop a couple of blocks down is a wealth of knowledge. He might help you more than a book ever could."

"Thanks. I can't believe I didn't think of talking with Smitty. I'll definitely do that." Faith smiled.

Once Faith had paid and left, Lou observed the disgruntled woman, wondering if she was going to have to call in for Easton's assistance to get her out of the bookshop. But it seemed she really wasn't lying about her allergies, and finally her nose got too stuffed up and her eyes too red, and she left.

But not more than a few minutes went by before there was yet another woman standing near the register, wringing her hands nervously.

Oh no, Lou thought with an inward groan. *Another disgruntled customer?*

"Good morning. How can I help you?" Lou asked in a

singsong voice as if being overly nice might save her from another verbal lashing.

"I'm hoping you can ..." The woman leaned closer. "It's just a little embarrassing to admit."

Frowning, Lou took a step closer and tipped her head so the woman wouldn't have to speak loudly.

"I hear you take cats and find them new homes." The woman spat out the sentence, then took one step back so she could study Lou's reaction.

"I do." Lou overcompensated with a big smile, hoping to put the nervous woman at ease.

"We bought a cat a couple of weeks ago from a breeder. She's gorgeous. We've never had a cat before, and we just love her." The woman's face crumpled into a scowl as she prepared for the next part. "What we didn't realize was how allergic to cats my son was." She shook her head. "He's in constant discomfort, and I have to find a new home for her."

Lou's still-guarded demeanor softened, seeing how heart-broken the woman was—not only for her son but also for herself. It was obvious from the way her eyes lit up as she talked about the cat that she loved her deeply.

The woman exhaled definitively. "It's awful, but we can't possibly keep Peaches. If you wouldn't mind, we'd love to drop her off here for you to rehome her."

"I would be happy to help." Lou held her hand out. "I'm Lou. What's your name?"

"Peggy Olsen." The woman took Lou's hand and shook it. "My son's name is Brian."

"Whenever you want to bring Peaches by, I'll be here. And if your son or anyone in your family wants to come visit Peaches, you're more than welcome to." If Brian was as allergic as he sounded, stepping foot inside Whiskers and Words might not be the best plan, but she had meant the invitation more for

Peggy. Lou could tell Peggy was going to be the one who had the hardest time letting go of the cat.

Peggy smiled, a little of the sadness and worry leaving her face. She had a pleasant smile when it wasn't pulled tight with nerves. "I—we would like that very much. Thank you, Lou. I'll go get her ready and be right back."

Lou waved goodbye. Once Peggy was gone, Lou pulled out her cell phone to call Noah, the local veterinarian. While she was sure the cat was healthy if Peggy had gotten it from a breeder, all of her other cats had gone through routine examinations with Noah, and Lou noticed how much it meant to prospective adopters when she mentioned they were all in perfect health. She pressed the call button and held the phone to her ear.

"I think you might be psychic. I was just going to call you," he answered in lieu of a greeting.

Lou laughed. "Shhh. The first rule of being psychic is that we're not supposed to talk about it."

Noah chuckled, saying, "Then those TV psychics are really doing it wrong. Anyway, what's up?"

"Oh, I have a new foster coming in later today. I was wondering if I could bring her by after closing so you can do an exam," Lou said.

"Or I could swing by," he suggested. "That might be less stressful on her. Anyone I would know?"

Lou wrinkled her nose. "I'm not sure. Do you know Peggy Olsen? She said they bought a cat from a breeder, but her son is allergic."

"Hmmm ... I know of Peggy, but hadn't heard they got a cat." Noah's tone was a little tight, and she wondered if it frustrated him that Peggy hadn't brought the cat in for a checkup.

After a few beats of silence, Lou asked, "Why were you about to call me?"

"Oh, maybe it's moot now that you're already getting a new foster ..."

"What?"

"Well, I have a stray someone brought in this morning. He's a little banged up and needs a cozy place to recuperate. I was wondering if the bookstore would be an option, but I understand if two new cats is too much."

"That wouldn't be too much at all," Lou said, excitement lifting her pitch. "The more the merrier."

Noah laughed. "Thank you. He has to stay here overnight since he had surgery today, but I can bring him over in the morning, and I'll examine the new cat for you then."

"Sounds good," Lou said, noticing Peggy was already walking down the street toward the shop. "I've got to go, Noah. I'll see you in the morning." She hung up the call and took in the sight in front of her.

After hearing that Peggy only had the cat for a couple of weeks, Lou expected Peaches to be a kitten, closer to three months old, but the cat Peggy carried into the bookshop was full grown. Full grown and *gorgeous*. She was a Rag Doll, a breed Lou had never heard of, but which looked like a fluffy Siamese.

Lou had planned to ask Peggy to keep Peaches separate from the other cats until Noah could examine her, but the woman carried the cat in her arms, without a crate or anything. The moment Peggy stepped inside, the cat launched herself out of Peggy's arms. She slipped under a chair in the corner, and when Peggy tried to pry her out, Peaches merely hid under a different piece of furniture.

"You can leave her out. It seems like she's fine with the other cats." Lou waved a dismissive hand at Peggy. She could try luring Peaches with food after she closed that evening and the shop was quieter. The other cats approached Peaches warily, but they all seemed to get along. Lou turned her attention back to Peggy. "Do you have any vaccination history for her?" Lou asked.

The woman shook her head. "Our breeder said she did all the vaccinations for us. And she said we didn't need to do any checkups because she was basically a vet after all these years of being a breeder."

Lou held back a frown. She seemed to remember there being vaccinations Sapphire had needed after they adopted him, but Peaches was older. The fact that all of her other cats were up to date on their vaccines gave her peace of mind. They would be protected and wouldn't pass anything on to Peaches. Still, Lou added it to her list of topics to discuss with Noah in the morning.

"Okay, well ... I'd better get going." Peggy left almost as quickly as she'd come, and Lou was sure she saw a tear drop down the woman's cheek.

Studying the newest arrival, Lou smiled as she lurked about the bookshop, exploring her new home. The other cats followed behind, interested. Even Sapphy got up from his nap in the midday sun to follow the fluffy cat as she sniffed out every corner. Lou tried to show her where the litter boxes were as well as the water and food, but Lou's proximity had proven to be too much, and the cat tucked herself away in the corner for the rest of the afternoon.

"We need a literary name for our newest arrival," Lou said to the cats once she'd closed up the shop for the day. She tapped her fingers against her lips as she thought.

Lou wasn't sure if it was because of the cat's fancy appearance, because of the ruined mansion on Thread Lane, or because she'd just finished *Great Expectations* the night before, but she thought of the tragic Miss Havisham, wearing her wedding dress for the rest of her life.

"What about Miss Clawvisham?" Lou asked the new cat,

craning her neck to catch a glimpse of her under a chair. The cat blinked her large eyes but remained in her hiding place. "Well, it doesn't seem like a no, so I'm going to take it."

The other cats were absolutely taken with the new arrival, to the point that Sapphire was the only cat who followed Lou upstairs at the end of the night. Lou didn't push it and left the rest of the cats in the shop, feeling better that Noah would be there in the morning.

He texted bright and early Monday morning, and Lou met him downstairs just as the sun rose. Noah carried a cat crate into the shop, set it down on the table next to Lou, and gestured to a tortoise-shell cat inside.

"He did well overnight, and his ear is healing nicely already, but I would still keep him separated from the other cats for a few more days." Noah glanced around, obviously searching for the other new foster.

"Aww. Sweet little guy." Lou opened the metal door of the crate and leaned down so she could get a better look at him. "You have had a rough go of it, haven't you?"

Besides a bandaged ear, the cat was scrawny. His tail was kinked in a way that made him look off center, and his eyes were a little uneven.

"He's a bit of a street urchin. But he's sweet," Noah said.

Lou pulled him out of the crate and cradled him in her arm. Noah was right. He was very sweet. The cat kneaded his paws into her shoulder and sank into her embrace.

"What are you going to name him?" Noah asked.

Lou had a few boy names ready to go, but based on the name she'd chosen for Miss Clawvisham, another Dickens-inspired name came right to her. It must've been Noah's use of the phrase "street urchin."

"The Artful Clawdger." Lou scratched the little guy's head. "And meet Miss Clawvisham." Lou placed Clawdger back into the crate as the newest arrival slipped out from under her hiding spot. Lou wasn't surprised; Noah had a calming way around people and animals alike.

"Gorgeous Rag Doll. I don't see many of these." Noah held out his hand as he slowly approached the new cat.

"Why are they called Rag Dolls?" Lou asked.

Noah smirked. "I'll show you." He knelt and picked up Miss Clawvisham. The cat went limp in his arms, like a stuffed animal toy.

"Ah." Lou laughed.

Noah set the cat on the table, and Lou moved Clawdger's crate so there was room for Noah to examine the new cat. The first thing he did was run a microchip reader over her front legs. A frown pulled at his normally cheerful expression.

"She's not microchipped. Did Peggy say anything about vaccinations?" Noah ran a hand over the back of his neck.

Lou repeated what Peggy had told her about the breeder.

Noah's jaw clenched tight.

"You don't think she vaccinated them?" Lou asked.

Noah shrugged. "Most breeders I know are great. But there are a few out there who try to cut corners by doing things themselves, and while *sometimes* they do it right, others aren't as good. Maybe I can call Peggy and get the name of the person she bought her from."

"Or I can. Let me know," Lou said.

Noah nodded distractedly as he observed Miss Clawvisham. "More pressingly, this cat has fleas, Lou."

Lou gasped but saw what Noah was talking about right away. She chided herself for not noticing earlier. "Omigosh, Peggy dropped her off without a crate, and then the cat hid, and I didn't even think to check." Lou let out a low groan. "And she's been around the other cats since lunch yesterday."

Noah smiled encouragingly. "It's okay. The wood floors in here are a good deterrent."

But Lou caught Anne Mice and Catnip Everdeen scratching at the same moment. She groaned again. "I don't have any of them on flea meds, Noah. I figured they'd be fine since they're all indoor cats, and we don't have dogs coming and going." She was used to Sapphire, who'd never needed to be on flea meds because he was always an indoor-only cat.

"It's okay," Noah said, but she could tell he was making a list of things they needed to do. "Okay, first things first. We need to get the Artful Clawdger isolated, so he doesn't get them too. I just got him flea free, so I don't want him to be infected again."

Following directions, Lou moved Clawdger to the back room, letting him have the run of the space while they took care of the rest of the cats. Lou put a note on the front door apologizing, but saying the store would be closed for the day. She'd planned on closing early to go grab her nieces from the airport, and had been using Mondays and Tuesdays—her slowest sales days—as days off, so it wouldn't be a big surprise to customers.

That taken care of, Lou steamed the furniture and ran a vacuum through the space while Noah ran to grab flea treatment and a special shampoo. He was a champ as he took the lead in giving each of them baths in the large sink in the back room. The angry, damp cats glared at him as they scratched.

By the time they were all done, Noah had to run to a midmorning appointment. Lou moved the cats upstairs, closed the bedroom doors, and prayed the flea medicine would do its job. Then she got to work, repeating the cleaning ritual she'd performed in the shop on her furniture upstairs, washing all of her bed linens as well since Sapphire had slept up there with her last night.

Finally finished, Lou collapsed on her couch. It was then

that she remembered she had to pick up her nieces at the airport in a few hours. Willow would arrive any minute to pick her up.

"A great time to have guests over, huh?" she asked the cats with a chuckle. And then she closed her eyes until Willow honked her horn, startling Lou awake.

CHAPTER 7

L ou locked the bookshop behind her and sank into the passenger seat of Willow's car. Her whole body screamed with fatigue.

"What's wrong with you?" Willow asked, poking Lou's arm as if she wasn't sure if she were alive.

"Fleapocalypse," Lou grumbled before explaining what had happened with Miss Clawvisham and her fleas.

"Do you think Peggy realized her cat had fleas?" Willow asked, eyes trained on the road as she drove.

Lou snapped her fingers. "Oh, thanks for reminding me. I was going to call her and let her know." Lou fished her phone out of her purse and typed in the number Peggy had left with her in case she had questions. "I sure hope she didn't know about the fleas," Lou said before pressing the call button.

But Peggy didn't answer, causing Willow to raise an eyebrow in suspicion and click her tongue.

Lou ignored her friend and left a message for Peggy, letting her know her cat had fleas, and she would probably need to treat her house since they had likely infested there as well.

Once that was taken care of, Lou sat back and sighed. "Thank you for driving," she said, smiling over at Willow.

Lou had yet to purchase her own car, never having the use for one in New York City. She was finding the same to be true here in the small town of Button, where she could walk pretty much everywhere she needed to go. There were times, like this, where a car would be nice to own. Luckily, Willow was free and was just as excited as Lou about the nieces arriving, so she'd volunteered to drive.

"Anytime," Willow said, pushing her shoulders back into the seat. "So, are all the fleas gone after your day of cleaning?"

Lou shook her head. "I've vacuumed and steam cleaned all of my furniture just in case, but since we just did their flea treatments, it could take another couple days for the cats to be flea free, so I can't let them back into the shop just yet."

"You should change your sign to Just Words, for Now," Willow said with a chuckle.

"Tell me about it. When that woman came in and yelled at me yesterday, I got to wondering if having a bookshop full of cats was a good business plan. Maybe this will be a way to find out." The thought left an uneasy feeling in Lou's stomach.

Willow must've noticed because she changed the subject. "Oh, I thought of something we could do each year for Ben's birthday celebration."

Lou shifted in her seat. Given everything happening with the murder investigation, the fleas, and her impending visitors, she'd totally forgotten to come up with ideas to commemorate Ben's birthday. Ever grateful for her caring best friend, Lou nodded for Willow to share her idea.

"You two always used to take those trips around his birthday each year. Why don't we keep that tradition going?" Willow suggested.

Free Trips, they used to call them. Not because they were

free of cost, but they were free of plans. A Free Trip had been Lou's gift to Ben their very first year together, when they were broke college students. He was more of a spontaneous risk-taker, and Lou liked detailed plans. So she'd promised him a day where they just drove somewhere. The only expectation was to have fun and go wherever looked interesting.

The first Free Trip had been to Staten Island and back, because neither of them had ridden on the ferry at that point. After the first year, Ben made sure Lou knew how much he'd loved the gesture and told her that was exactly what he'd wanted for his birthday every year beyond that. The trips had only grown in extravagance and distance each year

Lou laughed. "You'd want to do that?"

After her initial surprise wore off, Lou realized that, of course, it would work. Along with their loud personalities, Ben and Willow also shared a love of spontaneity. Plus, Willow had summers off, so she could take a trip in July, no problem.

"Anything for you." Willow chuckled, showing Lou it wasn't really a hardship for her. Even so, Lou knew the statement was as true as anything.

"It's a plan. And we can start with a trip with the girls while they're here." A lightness moved through Lou at the thought.

She'd spent so much time lately feeling anxious about forgetting Ben. Had moving away from New York made it too easy for her to stop picturing him, remembering the places they visited together? She'd worried that selling their condo had been a rash decision. But continuing traditions like the Free Trip felt right. Hanging on to the feelings and emotions Ben brought into her life was how she wanted to remember him, not with possessions.

Directions and traffic became the priority as they closed in on the airport. Anticipation built inside Lou as she got updates via text from her nieces about their plane landing and where they were waiting outside.

Willow pulled up to the arrivals section of the airport, and Lou scanned the crowd for the familiar faces of her nieces.

"There," Lou said, pointing about two hundred feet ahead where two lanky teenage girls stood, searching the line of cars in the same way Lou had just been doing to the people.

Mia, the sixteen-year-old, was a good three inches taller than she'd been at Ben's funeral last summer, and Maddy, seventeen now, wore eyeliner and practically looked like an adult.

Willow pulled over, popping the trunk as Lou unbuckled and slid out of the car.

The girls squealed, jumping up and down as Lou ran toward them. All of her fatigue from earlier was forgotten as excitement took over.

"Auntie Lou," they said in unison, crashing into her.

She pulled them into a quick hug, all three of them melting together for one sweet second before the hubbub of the airport and the whistles of traffic directors cut through their greeting.

"I'm so glad you're here." Lou stepped back and beamed at her nieces before motioning toward the car. "I'll get your bags."

While the girls crammed into the back seat, Lou put their bags in the trunk and then slid into the passenger seat. Willow saw an opportunity to pull into traffic and gunned it as Lou clicked her seat belt back into place and turned to admire the girls.

"How was your flight?" Lou asked.

"Fine," Maddy said, rolling her eyes like a seasoned traveler. As the eldest, she was further into her cynical teenage years and found regular life mundane at the best of times.

"Great," Mia said, giving a thumbs-up. Younger and more excitable, Mia's body language tightened with joy as she talked about the new Pixar movie they'd watched during the flight.

They spent the drive through the city catching up on what was new with the girls. Maddy was a barrel-racing champion with her faithful horse, Swift—she'd gotten the mare during the height of her Taylor Swift obsession in her early teens. They had made it through the local rodeo circuit and had made it to the state competition, set to take place a couple of weeks after they returned in August.

Mia, while still a recreational horseback rider, had fallen in love with downhill-ski racing and participated in the youth slalom competitions each winter.

Emily and Joe often talked about how lucky they were that the girls had chosen sports that competed in opposite seasons. Mia was back and forth to the local ski resort, Bridger Bowl, all winter, while Maddy had rodeos almost every weekend in summer.

Lou and Willow caught the girls up on how Lou's move had gone and how the bookshop was doing.

"What do you want to do while you're here?" Lou asked as the city fell away, and the lush vallies of Northern Washington filled the windows.

"Hang out with the cats, of course." Mia hunched her shoulders up by her ears.

Lou had introduced them to each of the cats via video in their most recent chat.

"But especially Sapphy," Maddy added seriously. She and Sapphire had always had a special bond.

During the nieces' first visit, after Ben and Lou had gotten Sapphire, Mia had still been young, all hands and tail pulling. But Maddy had been old enough to know how to be gentle with the cat, catering to his deafness in a way that had even Lou and Ben surprised, as if she just intuitively knew what he needed.

And whereas Sapphy was normally more of a napper, when Maddy was around, he followed her around like a puppy.

"Of course." Lou smiled. "And we have two new cats as of yesterday."

The girls leaned forward with interest as Lou told them about the Artful Clawdger and Miss Clawvisham.

"Unfortunately, they got fleas." Lou exhaled, hoping it wouldn't be too long before they would be in the clear. When the girls made worried faces, Lou held up a hand. "Don't worry. I'm not letting them in the bedrooms, and I steamed all the fabric surfaces. Noah assures me the fleas don't spread as much if you have wood floors, like I do in the apartment and the shop."

"Who's Noah?" Mia asked.

"The local veterinarian," Lou answered.

"And part-time sewer and handyman," Willow added.

The girls laughed.

"You'll like him. He's really nice, and his daughter, Marigold, is supersweet. She comes in to help with the cats a lot." Lou waited a beat before adding, "Any other requests for what you want to do while you're here?"

"Can we meet OC and Steve?" Maddy asked, to which Mia agreed with an emphatic head nod.

The girls had met Willow a few times throughout their lives, most recently at Ben's funeral. And while they'd heard about Willow's large chestnut gelding, they'd never met him, or Willow's newest addition, Steve the goat.

"Of course." Willow beamed. "Maddy, maybe you'll have to put him through his paces, see if he's got any barrel skills."

Willow mostly used an English saddle when she rode, but she had a western saddle that she used whenever she went on trail rides and wanted a little more to hang on to while on the trail.

"I also have a dressage competition this weekend, if you two are interested in coming with," Willow said, glancing at the girls in the rearview mirror.

They squealed with delight, the teenage equivalent of accepting the invitation.

After that, Lou and Willow took turns filling them in on the townspeople of Button. Lou thought about telling them about the murderer on the loose in town, but decided against it. She wasn't sure if Joey had shared the news with them and wanted to check with him first. The number of homeless people in Manhattan had appalled the girls when they'd last visited Lou and Ben. She didn't want to put a local murder on their empathetic consciences.

"We're taking you out to dinner tonight to celebrate," Lou said. "There are only four restaurants in town. So what do you feel like? Pizza? Barbecue? French cuisine? Or Thai?"

As the girls chatted about what they were hungry for, Lou contemplated her decision to keep the news of the murder from her nieces. She felt an intense need to protect them from the dangers of the world. Lou hoped she was just being overprotective and that they weren't really in any danger.

CHAPTER 8

Lou loved seeing the town of Button through her nieces' eyes as they pulled onto Thread Lane. In true teenage girl form, the girls awwed as they noticed the cute touches, from the sewing-themed street names to the brightly colored window frames most of the businesses featured, including the bookshop. Willow's pink flowering dogwood trees looked gorgeous in front of the shop, and Lou reminded herself to thank her friend once again for the loan.

"Here we are," Lou said, pride making her chest feel tight as they pulled in front of Whiskers and Words.

"Auntie Lou, it's so cute." Mia covered her mouth with a hand as she climbed out of the car.

Maddy stopped and turned toward Lou, tears crowding her eyes, causing her black eyeliner to smear. "Uncle Ben would've loved it."

Lou wrapped an arm around Maddy's shoulders—something that was getting harder as the girl grew. She pulled her close, and Maddy rested her head on Lou's.

"He would've, wouldn't he?" Lou held out her left arm and beckoned Mia to join them.

73

Willow, never one to be left out, swooped in from behind the group and wrapped them all in a tight hug with her lanky arms.

"Ooohff. Okay, Willow. I think that's tight enough," Lou wheezed.

The girls giggled, and the four of them retrieved the bags from the car and entered the bookshop.

The store smelled like heaven. The scent of new books and not-yet-cracked bindings sat heavy in the air in the satisfying way a heavy quilt settles over you in bed on a cold winter's night. The Artful Clawdger ran forward, meowing a lengthy greeting and rubbing up against their shins and the bags they held.

Mia and Maddy swooned over the scraggly cute cat, showering him with snuggles before Lou convinced them all to move upstairs. Seeing her apartment through their eyes was also a pleasant surprise. It wasn't as if she was ashamed of the small size of her new space—the first apartment she and Ben had shared in Brooklyn had been half its size. She'd been anxious that this life wouldn't seem satisfying or impressive enough and her nieces would worry she wasn't doing well in the wake of Ben's death.

But walking up the stairs and entering her home felt right. It was cozy, well-decorated, and looked—to Lou, at least—like a place anyone would be happy to spend their life. Willow took the girls' bags into the guest room.

"It's so cute, Aunt Lou." Maddy stretched her arms out as she took in the gas fireplace and soft gray couch.

"Kittens!" Mia squealed as the small herd of cats woke and came over and greeted the newcomers.

Maddy went straight for Sapphire while Mia sat on the floor and had three cats surrounding her as she laughed.

"Okay, what do you say we have dinner first, and then we

can come back here and spend all the time you can handle with these felines?" Lou suggested, her stomach rumbling a little, reminding her it was closing in on seven.

"Sounds good," Mia said, standing and brushing off the cat hair that had collected on her jeans.

"Did you decide on what you want to eat?" Lou asked, figuring they would choose the pizza place.

Maddy and Mia glanced at each other.

"The French place," Maddy said.

"Oh." Lou jerked her head back. She would've guessed the bistro was too fancy for the girls. But she supposed she needn't be surprised. The girls were on their way to becoming young women. She should've realized they wouldn't still be the little girls she remembered from their last visit. "Sure. It's really great."

Willow closed the guest bedroom door behind her after depositing the girls' luggage inside. "Their Chicken Cordon Bleu is to die for."

Lou's stomach grumbled again, agreeing with Willow's assessment. "Oh." She snapped her fingers together. "We should let your parents know you've gotten here safe and sound." Lou shook her head. "I completely forgot in all the excitement."

Maddy tapped the case of her cell phone. "I've already texted Dad like four times. He knows we're safe."

"Okay then," Lou said, marveling once more at how the girls were growing up. She distinctly remembered having to stay in touch with Joey and Emily during the girls' last visit because they would forget to communicate with their parents. And now she was the one forgetting.

The girls changed out of their airplane clothing, and then the foursome headed out to the Button Bistro. The sun was just dipping low enough in the sky that a beautiful peachy sunset spilled across the horizon.

Willow told Maddy and Mia the story of how she and Lou met in second grade, which Lou was pretty sure they'd heard at least three times already, but the girls listened with rapt attention. Lou's heart felt full as the teens' laughter spilled down the sidewalk ahead of them, surrounding her like a hug.

The bistro was hopping, which was to be expected on a summer evening, but they got a table by the window, which was perfect for people watching as well as catching the rest of the beautiful sunset.

Once they'd ordered, Lou let out a long sigh and smiled over at Mia and Maddy. "It's so good to have you two here."

Maddy pulled her mouth into a sad half smile. "We're so proud of you, Auntie Lou."

Mia nodded her agreement. "At first we were a little worried about you moving across the country without Uncle Ben." She breathed through the tightness in her throat that saying her uncle's name seemed to bring on. "But we can see this was exactly what you needed."

"And you have Willow here for you," Maddy added, smiling at Willow.

They relaxed into the evening, the girls chatting a million miles a minute about their friends and school. By the time their food arrived, Lou's stomach hurt but not from hunger. She couldn't remember laughing that hard in a while.

They'd just ordered dessert when Lou recognized a familiar person pass by on the street. George. She wore her usual ripped jeans and a baggy T-shirt with Princess Leia on it. Her long brown hair was in a messy bun on the top of her head. Lou waved to get her attention and motioned for her to come inside, before remembering that she hadn't seen George since she ran from the shop the other day.

The happiness surrounding her now that her nieces were here had caused her to momentarily forget. But the awkward smile George adopted as she walked inside was more than enough of a reminder.

"George, these are my nieces, Maddy and Mia," Lou said, trying to act normal. "Girls, this is a friend of ours, George."

"Like George Elliot?" Maddy asked, making Lou proud.

George smiled. "Exactly. It's great to finally meet the famous nieces," George said, proving Lou talked about them enough to make an impression with her regulars. "I didn't know you were visiting."

Of course she wouldn't have known about the girls coming to visit. She hadn't been by the bookshop since before Lou got the call from Joe, Lou realized with yet another spike of discomfort.

Unaware of any awkwardness, Maddy and Mia were transfixed with the older girl, and Lou could see from their sparkling eyes that she'd just earned some cool aunt points by having a friend like George. Though she suspected that calling them cool points would get them immediately revoked.

George's expression tightened. "I'd better get going," she said as their dessert, a New York-style cheesecake with chocolate sauce, showed up.

They waved goodbye as the teenagers attacked the dessert.

Willow leaned toward Lou. "Well, that was awkward," she whispered so the nieces might not hear.

"I know. She hasn't been to the shop since she ran out on Friday after I brought up the mansion," Lou explained. "I feel awful about bringing it up."

"You had no idea." Willow frowned.

"I guess, but if it was just my questions on Friday, I feel like she would be back." Lou wet her lips. "I think something else is

77

keeping her away. Do you think it could be because I was the one to find Ron?"

Maddy cleared her throat. "What are the two of you whispering about over there?"

Mia leveled them with an equally no-nonsense look. The fact that she had chocolate in the corner of her mouth made her a little less intimidating, but not much.

In the couple of hours she'd spent with her nieces so far, during this visit, the one thing she'd realized was how much more grown up they were than she remembered. They deserved to know what happened.

"A man was murdered on Tuesday, and I found him," Lou said.

To her surprise, Maddy said, "Oh yeah. Dad told us." Maddy took a big bite of cheesecake before adding, "But we didn't realize you were the one who found the body. Tell us everything."

Mia nodded. "We've been listening to true crime podcasts with Mom. We're hooked."

Lou shrugged. If Joe and Emily trusted them to hear that kind of stuff, she was sure they'd be okay hearing about her experience. So Lou explained what had happened, leaving out the gorier details.

"So all you know about the person who was at the scene was that they wore a dark hoodie?" Mia asked.

"They left shoe prints too," Lou said. "Their shoes had stars all along the soles."

At that, the girls coughed and looked at each other.

"What?" Willow asked.

"We know what kind of shoes those are," Maddy said. "They're called Five Points. They're really popular."

"I think you're definitely searching for a younger person," Mia explained.

"But that's Montana. They might not be popular with the younger population up here," Lou said thoughtfully.

"I think they are," Maddy said. "George was wearing a pair just now." She motioned to the place George had been standing just moments before.

Lou's stomach dropped. In that moment, she realized it might have been rash to assume George wasn't a suspect in the murder of Ronald Rossback.

CHAPTER 9

The noise and movement of the crowded bistro pulsed around Lou as she digested what her niece had just said.

It was only then—too late—that she remembered where she'd seen the star pattern on the bottom of someone's shoes before.

Whereas Silas and Forrest usually sat on the couch and love seat in the bookshop when they visited, George often plopped right onto the floor, loving when the cats swarmed around her. Seated like that, the bottoms of her shoes were visible. She'd worn the Five Points, as Lou's nieces had called them, and Lou thought she wore them often.

"George was wearing the star shoes?" Willow asked, frown lines deepening on her forehead. She swallowed, and Lou knew she was thinking of how they'd crossed George's name off the list of suspects in Ronald's murder.

Maddy, unaware of the implications, nodded. "Yeah, my friend Jenna has the same teal pair George had on just now."

Willow's fingers closed over Lou's arm, gripping tight as the nieces turned their attention back to the dessert. "Should we tell Easton?"

Lou flinched at the suggestion. "I'm sure he already knows. If they're a popular brand, he's been able to find out that younger people wear them. It's not like George is hiding that she owns a pair. He knows about her connection to the accident."

"Who's Easton?" Mia asked, thankfully not focusing on what Lou had said about George.

"He's a detective, and Willow's neighbor," Lou explained.

"And he's insufferable," Willow added with an eye roll.

The girls shared a smirk but leaned back over the dessert.

"Easton is also a good detective. He's got this case covered." Lou shot a pointed look at Willow, who put her hands up in concession.

But even though she convinced Willow to drop the idea of getting involved in the investigation, Lou was riddled with doubts.

That night, when they'd returned home after dinner, and the girls had gone to bed, tired from their flight, Lou stayed up. Tired as she was from her day of washing cats and steam cleaning, she couldn't sleep. A shadow hung over her thoughts.

The case had felt close enough to Lou already, having been the one to find Ron's body. But the realization that George might have been involved made Lou's head and heart hurt simultaneously. Was that why George had been avoiding Lou and the bookshop since Friday?

Creeping out of bed so she wouldn't wake the girls in the guest bedroom next door, Lou grabbed her laptop from the coffee table in the living room and brought it into her bedroom, closing the door she usually left cracked open for the cats.

Lou typed in Ronald Rossback's name. She wasn't sure what she was looking for, but the first thing that came up was his obituary in the local paper. Besides a vague description of his death, it mentioned that there would be a small graveside service tomorrow at noon.

Graveside? Lou's heart hurt. She supposed with everyone around hating him, there wasn't anyone who would want to throw him a proper memorial. She resolved to go.

The next morning, she woke early and was texting back and forth with Willow while she prepped her coffee and breakfast for the girls. When Lou spilled the news about Ron's graveside service to her, Willow had offered to take the girls for the day so Lou could go. They had everything figured out, so by the time the teenagers stumbled blearily from the guest bedroom, Lou met them with pancakes and a big smile.

"What do you think about going over to Willow's today to spend time with her, OC, and Steve?" Lou asked, trying not to sound too eager. She may have been okay talking to her nieces about the case, but she definitely didn't feel okay taking them to a graveyard.

As it turned out, she needn't have worried. The girls were so excited with the prospect that they almost didn't want to eat, let alone ask questions about what Lou might be doing with her day. But after making sure they got a couple of pancakes each in their stomachs, Lou released them to get ready.

Willow picked them up a little while later, pulling up in front of the bookstore and beeping her horn. She waved a greeting to Lou as the girls rushed out and climbed into the car.

By the time lunch came around, Lou closed the shop, leaving a sign on the front door letting customers know she would be closed for about an hour. She hoped that would be enough time.

The cemetery was south of Button Lake. Lou left early, giving herself more than enough time, which turned out to be a good thing because by the time she got there, there were only five minutes to spare before noon. It took Lou seven minutes to locate the grave of Ronald Rossback. She found an open grave and modest casket. A man stood next to the opening in the earth, his head bowed forward.

She studied the man as she approached, her sandals sinking into the soft grass around the plots of land where bodies were laid to rest. The man next to Ronald's grave site was about her height, maybe a little taller, and he wore a dark gray suit that fit him so well it had to have been individually tailored to fit his body. Between the quality fit of the suit and his fancy silk tie, Lou guessed the man had money. He had a small bald patch on the crown of his head, visible through his thinning brown hair, and she noticed the rest of it was cropped short, probably in response to its thinning state.

He glanced up, noticing movement, and his eyes flashed with surprise. "Oh, I'm sorry. You startled me a bit."

"Didn't expect anyone else to show?" Lou asked.

The man exhaled a humorless laugh. "Not really. To be honest, I wasn't even sure if I should come. I don't know if I believe that Ronald can tell if anyone came, but I wanted to say goodbye."

"How did you know him?" Lou asked quietly, feeling like anything above a whisper would disrupt the eerie quiet that surrounded them in the graveyard.

"I was his lawyer." The man turned to her and held out a hand. "Jeff Jeffries."

Lou shook his hand, and worked really hard to keep her facial expression neutral even though his name would've normally made her giggle.

"I know," Jeff said with a chuckle. "My parents thought they were being clever. At least it's easy to remember for my clients."

Lou smiled. "I'm Louisa. You can call me Lou. So you were his lawyer?" she asked as she took in the title.

Somehow, the fact that the only person other than her to show up to Ron's burial was his lawyer stung even more. Lou wasn't sure if the man really deserved her pity, though. Button was her new home. The people had welcomed her with open arms. She felt protective of them, and if this man hurt them, maybe it was better for everyone that he was gone.

"Lawyer and friend," Jeff added after a moment.

Lou's lips parted as she inhaled, surprised by this addition.

Noticing her disbelief, Jeff said, "I don't know what you've heard about him, but I can assure you he wasn't as bad as everyone around here made him out to be. How did you know him?"

Lou shook her head. "I didn't. I'm the one who found him, though."

After a quick elevation of his eyebrows, Jeff said, "And you obviously don't believe all the stories they tell about him around here."

His words cut to a truth she hadn't wanted to admit. "You knew him. You don't think he was a bad person?"

Jeff shrugged. "He wasn't perfect, that was for sure. But he also wasn't as callous as they told themselves. They needed someone to blame, though. There were a lot of things that factored into the accident that day."

Lou listened, eager to hear a different side of the story than what she'd heard from the other locals. If she'd learned anything from her days as an editor, there was always another side to each story. Sometimes she'd read a manuscript and think one thing, only to find out the author meant to convey a completely different message.

Jeff continued his story. "I've heard the stories about Ronald being lazy and not taking care of the steel mill after he inherited it. He did his best. By the time his father passed on the business, the American steel industry was already on a downward trajectory. More and more, companies were opting to outsource their steel, and the American mills couldn't match their prices." Jeff sighed. "I urged Ron to close the business immediately once he took over, something his father was too stubborn to do, but he said he wanted to stay open as long as possible for the local workers, even if it meant him losing money each year."

Lou nodded along with the story. She'd never been in a business where she needed to know much about steel, but she'd definitely heard the problem Jeff was talking about mentioned on the news regarding the economy. The effect the mills closing around the country had on local communities was devastating, and that was without the horrific accident that preceded Tinsdale's closure.

"Ron spent as much as he could on maintenance, but the money was running out. Workers were leaving, tired of the conditions, and the night of the accident, many of the workers present had been pulling double shifts to make up for the loss." Jeff stared off into the distance for a second, as if reliving the moment he heard the news.

"But it was easier for the town to blame it all on Ron," Lou summarized, understanding where Jeff was going with his story.

"Yes," Jeff said. "And Ron never fought them when they made him into the scapegoat. He knew he could be that for them. It was one way he said he was making penance."

"One way?" Lou cocked her head.

"Well, the money was another big one," Jeff said. "He gave almost everything he had to the local charity fund the town set up after the accident for families of the victims."

"But they were still too angry to forgive him?" Lou guessed.

Jeff's shoulders tensed. "They never knew it was him. He had me do all the donations anonymously so they wouldn't know who'd made them. Ron either didn't want their forgiveness or didn't think he deserved it. "

A sad smile pulled at Lou's mouth as she regarded Ronald's grave. "Well, I'm glad that at least a couple of us know he wasn't as bad as everyone made him out to be."

"Yes, thank you for being here," Jeff said. "Telling you has brought me a sense of closure I didn't know I needed until now." He stretched his shoulders back as if they felt lighter. "I just wish Ron had gotten some of that."

Lou exhaled. She wished he could've too.

"It was nice to meet you, Lou." Jeff held out his hand. When Lou shook it, he straightened his lapels and said, "I'd better get back to the office." And with that, he was off.

As Jeff's outline moved away through the graveyard, Lou pondered what she'd just learned. A twig snapped, bringing Lou's focus back to the present. Easton moved to stand next to her.

"Hey," she said. "What are you doing here?"

Easton laughed. "I was about to ask you the same thing. You know, usually we come to funerals because the killer will often show up." He elbowed her, giving her a teasing smirk.

Lou smiled, but it dropped quickly into a frown. "His lawyer was here. You just missed him. Jeff Jeffries?"

"Already cleared," Easton said, catching her implied question. "He's got a solid alibi. Was in a court case that evening. Already checked into him."

"Makes sense." Lou relaxed. "He also seemed to be the only person who liked the guy." Lou turned to face Easton. "Did you know Ron donated almost all of his money to the local charity fund for the victims of the accident?"

Easton nodded. "Though, I only just found out when I pulled his financial records and realized the guy was broke and had been for decades."

Lou's gaze moved back to the coffin and the machine that would soon lower it into the ground. She wrung her hands in front of her guiltily for a moment before blurting, "Easton, the star shoe print we found outside, the one from the person who fled the scene ... George has those same shoes." Lou grimaced as the words left her mouth. "My nieces recognized them right away. They're popular with teens, I guess."

"George has an alibi. She was with her grandparents." Easton kept his eyes forward. His face was still, but Lou could tell he was chewing on the information she'd just given him. Easton ran a hand over his face. "They've got me piled on with the cases right now. I haven't even had time to get ahold of Aiden Foreman yet, and he's around George's age, so maybe he's got those shoes too. The police chief, like the rest of the town, wasn't the biggest fan of Ron's, so he's not giving me a lot of help."

"Almost as if they don't care if his murder is solved or not." That didn't sit right with Lou.

Was Easton telling her because he wanted her to get involved? Did he want her to do what he couldn't? What his chief wasn't letting him?

Instead of saying anything else, Easton raised a hand in a wave and walked away, leaving Lou alone by Ronald's grave.

Lou stayed there for a few more minutes. She stayed partly because she wanted to honor Ron. She wasn't sure what kind of honor the man deserved. Jeff had a very different opinion of the man, but maybe he was the only one who truly knew him. Lou felt strongly that he deserved more than just his lawyer knowing his true character. Lou also stayed because she was enjoying the way the cool breeze drifted through the leaves of the oak trees dotting the small graveyard.

And then someone walked up and stood next to Lou.

For a moment, she thought it was Easton, returned to give

her his full blessing to work the case he was too busy to look into. But then Lou caught sight of the sneakers on the feet of the person standing next to her.

Five Points.

She slowly glanced up into the eyes of George.

CHAPTER 10

George stood next to Lou at Ronald's grave, her hands shoved deep into her jeans pockets. The stiffness to her posture advertised how uncomfortable she was.

Lou wasn't sure whether it was hearing that George had an alibi or because she'd been spending too much time with Willow, but her first reaction was to pull George into a tight hug.

She didn't know why George was there, but at that moment, it didn't matter. Ron was proof that sometimes people needed a person to think the best of them.

"Oof." George exhaled forcefully and then laughed. She wrapped her arms around Lou, though considerably less tightly, until Lou let go. "So ... you know why I ran out of the bookshop that day?" George asked quietly as Lou stepped away.

Lou puffed out her cheeks. "I do. I'm so sorry. It was insensitive of me to bring it all up, especially this week."

George gave Lou an exasperated glower. "Lou, you are the least insensitive person I know. You didn't know what happened, so how were you supposed to know to avoid the subject?" She shook her head. "I'm fine. My dad died when I was two. My mom even before that. I never knew them enough to miss them." She sniffed, playing it off as an itch on her nose, but Lou could see her eyes becoming watery.

"How are you doing?" Lou wrapped an arm around her shoulders, a little difficult, considering they were just about the same height.

George snorted. "Honestly?"

Lou nodded. "Willow and I have this thing we say when we want to check in on each other. We say honest three. The other person has to list the first three emotions they're feeling. The only rule is that you can't overthink what you feel. There are no judgments in honest three." Lou trained her eyes on George. "And that's what I'm asking ... honest three?"

George rubbed the heel of her hand against her temple. "Relieved, heartbroken, happy." George flinched at the last one.

"Nope," Lou scolded her. "There are no judgments, so there's no shame in how you feel."

"It's crazy that I still feel heartbroken after all this time," George said.

Lou was only about a year out from the biggest loss of her life, but she couldn't ever imagine the heartbreak going away. Lessening? Sure. But it wouldn't ever be totally gone.

"Which means I'm relieved that Ronald is dead. I'm happy, actually. And that might make me a terrible person." George's eyebrows bunched together on her forehead as she scowled.

"I don't think it makes you terrible. It makes you human." Lou put a hand on George's shoulder.

George sighed. "Thanks. I wanted to come talk to you, to explain everything after I ran out of the shop that morning, but then I heard about the murder, and how you were the one to find him and ..." She puffed out her cheeks. "I didn't know what to say." She let out a quick laugh. "I paced in front of the bookshop so much, I was sure you were going to spot me and tell me to come inside. I think maybe I was hoping you would."

Relief flooded Lou's thoughts, erasing some of her worries. It had been George's shoe prints in front of the shop that day. It had been George waiting for the courage to go inside and talk to Lou, not the murderer.

"Why were you scared to talk to me?" Lou asked.

"We'd gone for so long without talking about Ron," George said, "about what happened. It felt wrong to start." She paused. "Do you remember when you invited me over for dinner that first time and you were telling me about losing Ben?"

Lou nodded. "I feel awful that I didn't ask you what kind of pain you were hiding. It was the perfect opportunity, and I only saw my loss."

"That's not why I brought that up," George said. "I don't want you to feel badly about that. I should've said something then. But it's like you said that night. You wanted to keep talking about Ben, for people to not be afraid to bring him up around you. You didn't want him to become an unpleasant topic, something that was off limits." She pressed her lips together. "That's exactly what happened with my dad, with the accident, with Ron, and that stupid house," she scoffed.

Lou's heart ached at the realization of what the imposed silence had stolen from George, from all the victims of the accident. Sure, maybe it had placed a bandage over the wound at first. Maybe it made it easier to not think about or talk about the difficult thing that happened.

Lou knew, firsthand, how difficult it was to confront those feelings, those truths she didn't want to accept, especially at first.

But if she hadn't, she wouldn't be able to heal.

George hadn't been allowed to heal properly. A tear fell down her cheek. "Like I said, I was so young when he died. I don't have any actual memories of him. My grandparents told me stories and talked about him." She held up a hand in case Lou thought she hadn't ever been able to talk about the man. "They showed me pictures and told me stories all the time about my dad and my mom. But I would love to hear from the rest of the town, as well. They knew my parents so well, and they really shied away from talking about them. I know it was their way of trying to protect me, but ..." She drifted off, punctuating the thought with a shrug.

Lou wasn't sure if it was the fact that her nieces were visiting, or if she'd just never seen the confident George so vulnerable, but a maternal instinct washed over her. The need to protect her and help her see that everything was going to be okay overwhelmed her.

"I don't think it's too late at all," Lou said, giving George's shoulder a squeeze. "People are already talking about what happened more than ever because of what happened to Ronald. Maybe you could use the opportunity to tell them what you need."

George sniffed. "I think I could do that."

Lou studied her out of the corner of her eye. "You could let that be something nice Ron has done for you. His death can give you an opening to tell the people around you the truth," she suggested, anxious about how George would take the intimation that Ron did anything right.

George gave Lou a small smile. "I think I can thank him for that." She swiped a finger under each eye. "You know, I came here today because I thought it would make me feel happy to see him dead, finally. And it did, at first." She wrinkled her nose. "But now I just feel kind of sad. I don't know if I believe anyone is completely bad, so I hope that as he lived the last twenty years of his life, he made amends for what he did."

"I think he tried," Lou said.

They stood there for a few more minutes, but as if they could both feel it was time, they turned to leave.

"Do you have to get back to your place, or do you want to get coffee and come hang out at the bookshop with me and the newest cat?" Lou asked, an excited smile peeling across her face as George's demeanor changed.

George's shoulders lifted. "A new cat?"

"Well, there are two, actually. But only one is allowed in the shop at the moment." Lou gave George a look that told her it was a long story. "He's a little rough around the edges, but he's got a heart of gold."

"I definitely need to come meet him. Staying away from the bookshop for the past few days has been torture." She laughed.

Lou elbowed her. "Well, it's good to have you back."

Together, they walked back to Whiskers and Words.

CHAPTER 11

In some ways, the next day seemed like everything was back to normal. George returned in the morning, meaning all three of Lou's regulars were back in the bookshop together. But the differences in the shop that day were still undeniable.

For one, Lou's nieces were spending the day in the bookshop. And while their presence was lovely, it added a different dynamic to the space. Lou introduced Mia and Maddy to Silas and Forrest, as they'd already met George. And while an air of awkwardness hung in the space for the first few moments after opening, they settled into a comfortable conversation. Forrest was especially good at getting the girls talking, asking questions about their hobbies back home in Montana. And even though Lou could see the admiration the girls had for George, it was Silas who they really latched on to. Maddy seemed to love his grumpy attitude, and Mia giggled each time he vocally harrumphed.

The other difference that morning was that there were still no cats in the shop besides the Artful Clawdger. When Silas and

Forrest saw there was only one cat, their excitement visibly deflated.

"The new cat gave them all fleas. They're upstairs until I can make sure they are flea free," Lou explained.

"That one gave them all fleas?" Silas asked, pointing to Clawdger. "Why doesn't he have to be locked away upstairs?"

"Not him," Lou said, feeling defensive of the scrappy guy. "Another new cat came in, and I didn't realize she had fleas."

Silas cleared his throat. "Are you sure? Because this one here looks like he's made of fleas."

George jumped to his rescue, having spent time with him yesterday. She patted his head and said, "I think he's kind of cute."

Mia and Maddy nodded, frowning at Silas. Lou had never seen him care about what anyone thought about him, but having her nieces scowl disapprovingly at him seemed to change his attitude and he softened.

Lou smiled down at Clawdger. "He is cute, and he's very sweet. He just needs a nice safe place to call home."

They settled into their normal routine, Lou working on stocking and organizing the shelves while chatting with the regulars and her nieces. Eventually, Silas, George, and Forrest left to get on with their other business, and the girls lost themselves in books. They asked Lou if she needed any help, but she was much happier seeing them kicked back with a book in their hands. She could handle the workload of the bookshop alone. It was what she did everyday, after all.

There was one thing that grated on her patience, however. The whole day Lou dealt with customers asking where all the cats were and then scowling at the lone, raggedy feline. She was considering following Willow's advice and typing up a sign that said, *Just Words For Now*. That way she wouldn't have to keep answering the same question, but also, maybe people wouldn't come in only to be disappointed and leave.

The one positive outcome was that it showed Lou, without a doubt, how much of a draw the cats were to her customers, and put to rest the doubts that had cropped up after the angry woman's allergic rant the other day.

As happy as she was that people asked about the other cats, Lou couldn't help but feel bad for the Artful Clawdger. His scrappy appearance probably wouldn't have been so alarming, or noticeable, if he hadn't been the only one in the shop. Because the little guy was spotlighted, everyone saw him in all his scratched and scarred glory.

Lou was snuggling with him on the couch right before closing while Mia and Maddy were upstairs taking a break, when the front door opened. Noah's ex-wife, Cassidy, walked inside with their daughter, Marigold. They held two fleece cat beds and wore wide smiles.

"Noah said you had two recent additions who might need beds." Cassidy handed the bed she held to Marigold, and the girl brought them both over to Lou. In explanation, Cassidy said, "I'm going to keep my distance since I think if I get within five feet of that little guy, I won't be able to stop sneezing."

"Understandable. Thank you." Lou beamed as she gestured to the beds Marigold held.

Marigold and Noah had made fleece beds for each of the Whiskers and Words cats, giving them cozy napping spots around the shop, but also giving adopters something to bring home with them when they made one of the shop cats part of their family. It was a lovely gesture, one Lou had always felt was very heartwarming.

"I made these two all by myself this time," Marigold said, holding forward the beds as if they were great treasures.

Lou's eyes widened with appreciation. "Oh, that's wonderful."

Marigold had been the first to admit that Noah had done most of the work on the other beds. His family owned the local quilt shop, however, so Lou wasn't surprised that they would work with Marigold on sewing lessons as she got older.

Proving exactly why Lou adored the nine-year-old, Marigold squealed with delight at the sight of Clawdger and she immediately cuddled up with the scrappy cat, showing none of the hesitation most of the adults in town had at his appearance.

"He's so sweet. What's his name?" Marigold said.

"The Artful Clawdger. He's named after a crafty street kid in Charles Dickens's book *Oliver Twist*. The character's real name is Jack Dawkins, but I think the street name fits him better," Lou explained.

As if hearing the inspiration behind his name reminded him he had mischief to create, the cat jumped off the couch and batted at a sunbeam on the floor of the children's section. Marigold followed him.

Footsteps clomped down the stairs, and Lou's nieces came down into the bookshop.

"Girls, this is Marigold, who I was telling you about." Lou motioned to the little girl.

Marigold looked up from chasing Clawdger and gawked at the teenage girls. The awe that she wore in her expression was similar to the way Mia and Maddy had gaped at George. They walked over to the children's section and knelt next to Marigold, talking to her as they took turns petting the cat.

Seeing the girls were all occupied, Lou turned back to Cassidy.

But Cassidy spoke first. "I heard you had an interesting day on Friday."

Lou nodded, glancing up at the real estate agent. "Do you know who gets the house now that Ron is gone?" Lou asked, doubting the man had any family if he was such a loner.

To her surprise, Cassidy said, "He has a nephew. I'm assuming he'll sell, though."

Lou's eyes widened. Could Ron's nephew be a suspect? Had he murdered his uncle to get the house?

Cassidy seemed to understand what she was thinking, though, because she said, "He lives three states away. I'm sure Easton will check that he has an alibi, but the house isn't worth much in its current state. Definitely not enough to kill over."

"Oh," Lou said, digesting that information. "Do you think anyone will buy? It needs so much work."

Cassidy tipped her head to one side. "I had a buyer interested a couple of months ago, but knew Ron wouldn't even entertain the idea of selling, so my assistant told her not to even try. She might still be interested. Some people go around searching for places like that to gut and renovate."

Lou hoped the new owner would renovate rather than tear down the entire structure. She was sure the house had been beautiful at one time and could see it restored to its former glory if given time and dedication.

The front door to the shop opened, and in strode a large man. He wore a wide smile and had thick, close-cropped hair. Lou wouldn't call him a regular, but she'd seen him a few times over the last handful of months. He usually purchased westerns and had a thing for Louis L'Amour.

"Cassidy French, is that you?" The big man's booming voice echoed through the building. He stretched out his arms.

Cassidy turned around and beamed. "Derrick! How are you?" She sprang forward into the man's arms, his gigantic frame making her look almost childlike.

Pulling away, Derrick bobbed his head. "I'm fantastic. I

mean, how could I be anything else with Ron the scum finally out of our lives?" He moved on, like he'd just commented on the weather, instead of metaphorically dancing on a dead man's grave. "How's the kid?"

Cassidy's gaze moved to Lou in discomfort, and she must've decided not to acknowledge Derrick's comment about Ron because she gestured over to the children's section, where Marigold was still talking to Lou's nieces. "She's great. Growing like a weed."

Marigold waved at the tall man. Mia and Maddy studied him but eventually turned back to Marigold.

Cassidy put her hands on her hips and looked Derrick up and down. "Man, what has it been? Two years? How is that possible when we live in the same small town?"

"I've been working evenings. The schedule means I miss a lot of people." Derrick shrugged.

"Oh, I didn't realize." Cassidy cocked her head.

Derrick's rosy-cheeked smile faded a bit. He quickly added, "I was sorry to hear about you and Noah splitting."

Now it was Cassidy's turn for discomfort to spike through her posture, turning her spine rigid. She dropped her arms to her sides. Her gaze cut over to Lou, knowing she and Noah were friends. "Oh, it's fine. It's for the best."

Sensing Cassidy's discomfort, Lou waved and pointed over to the shop computer, miming that she had some work to get done. She left the two old friends to catch up in private.

But creating space between her and Cassidy didn't mean her thoughts left the topic alone. When Lou had first moved to town, she'd been surprised when she'd heard Noah and Cassidy were divorced. They were the perfect team, getting along better than any two divorced people than Lou had ever experienced. But Willow had filled her in on the real reason behind the couple's split: Cassidy forming feelings for a man she'd met at a regional real estate conference. Lou also knew that the peaceful relationship Cassidy and Noah shared now had been mostly because of Noah deciding to put any hurt he was feeling behind him and focus on what was best for his daughter. Lou couldn't imagine anyone deciding they didn't want to be with Noah. He was kind, gentle, and strikingly handsome. But she also knew the two had been together since high school, so maybe Cassidy had changed enough that she didn't feel like they fit any longer.

A few minutes later, Cassidy and Derrick hugged, punctuating their brief encounter. Mia and Maddy were on their phones on the couch, and Marigold was shopping for books. Cassidy went to find Marigold, and Derrick approached the checkout counter, a small trade paperback Western appearing even smaller than usual in his giant hands.

"Needed some new reading material." He tapped the book on his palm before handing it over to Lou to ring up.

She smiled as he paid. "Enjoy."

He thanked her and waved to Cassidy once more before leaving. He climbed into a lifted maroon truck with large tires. Its diesel engine roared to life, and he backed out of the parking spot before heading down the street.

"How do you know him?" Lou asked Cassidy, who was bringing a book to the register to buy for Marigold.

Cassidy grinned. "Derrick Hops? He and my dad are close. Derrick used to be the union president for the local steelworkers back in the day. My dad was one of the shift managers at the mill before it closed down."

Lou's jaw dropped open. "Wait. Your dad worked there during ...?" Lou couldn't seem to finish her question.

But she didn't need to. Cassidy knew what she meant. "He did. Thankfully, he managed the night shift at that point, so he wasn't even at the mill when the accident happened."

"Your family must've really despised Ron, then." Lou

chanced a quick glance at Cassidy. "How are you dealing with possibly having to sell his old house?"

Cassidy scoffed, "To be honest? Loving it. That man hurt a lot of people I loved. But my family wasn't hit too bad. My mom was an attorney, and she was able to support us while my dad found another job. He got a different job pretty quickly, unlike ... others." Cassidy peered over her shoulder in a way that made Lou sure Derrick had been in the latter group.

Lou realized that Silas had been right. It wasn't just the families of the workers who'd died in the accident who might've wanted revenge on Ron for what he'd done. And if Lou was putting together a suspect list, what Derrick had said about Ron when he'd first arrived earned him a place at the top.

"So your family still lives around here, then?" Lou asked, hoping this question would lead into the ones she really wanted to ask about Derrick.

Cassidy nodded. "My parents still live in the house I grew up in, over on Stitch Street. And my brother, Casey, lives in Brine. He's a police officer over there."

A smile pulled at Lou's lips at the mention of the town next door to Button. Willow had filled Lou in on the difference between the two small towns. Button was cute as a button, and Brine was as salty as their name suggested. They were the quirky alternative to Button, pulling in far fewer tourists each year. And even though there seemed to be an unspoken agreement in Button that Brine was to be looked down upon, Lou couldn't help but enjoy the funny little town.

"What about Derrick?" Lou asked, hoping she wasn't being too obvious. "I see him in the shop sometimes. Does he still live here? Was he able to get back on his feet?"

Cassidy's expression went slack. She wet her lips. "He still lives in Button."

For a moment, Lou thought Cassidy might try to avoid answering the second question altogether.

But then she said, "It took Derrick a lot longer to find his place after the mill closed. He got so emotionally involved, helped each of the families out with lawsuits, and had a hard time moving on once it was all closed. He carried around a lot of hatred for Ron ... still does—did." Cassidy tipped her head toward the place they'd been standing when he'd brought up his relief at Ron's death.

Lou wasn't sure what to say. She could tell Cassidy wouldn't be the one to ask about Derrick regarding Ron's murder. He was a close family friend, and she might be reluctant to paint him as a murderer. So Lou rang up the book Marigold had picked out and waved goodbye to the two as they left her alone in the shop with her nieces, still on their phones on the couch.

As soon as Cassidy and Marigold were out the front door, the girls vaulted up and rushed over to where Lou stood.

"Auntie Lou, that guy is bad news." Maddy turned her phone to show Lou a social media account. "After he said that stuff about him being glad Ron was dead, we looked him up online, and he's said a lot of nasty stuff about the dead guy."

Mia nodded. "A lot of it has been within the last month."

Lou scanned the screen in front of her and raised an eyebrow as her eyes pored over hateful post after hateful post. One of his posts called for Ron to *finally get what he deserved. Twenty years is long enough,* Derrick had written.

A shiver worked its way up Lou's spine. "But he just said he works evenings. He was probably at work when Ron was killed." Lou frowned as Maddy turned her phone screen back toward herself and scrolled through the posts again.

"Unless he was off that Friday. Or doesn't ever work Fridays," Mia suggested.

Lou thought about that. "True, but you saw that man. He

was huge. He definitely wasn't the person I saw running away from the mansion on Friday."

"Auntie Lou," Maddy said, her voice dropping into a serious register, "you at least owe it to yourself and Ron to mention this guy to Easton."

CHAPTER 12

Lou knew Maddy was right. She needed to tell Easton what she'd just heard Derrick say about Ronald's murder. She considered her nieces, wondering if she should take them with her.

"You should go alone, Aunt Lou," Maddy said, making the decision for her.

"We'll be fine," Mia added.

As if realizing that she would worry about leaving them there alone, Maddy added, "We'll lock the door behind you and won't let anyone in unless it's you."

Lou's mouth pulled into a grateful smile at her nieces' maturity. "Okay. Thank you. Be safe, you two." She blew a kiss at them before running out the door, heading down the street to the police station.

Lou picked up her pace as they crossed Thread Lane and then Binding Street to get to the police station. Lou had only been inside a handful of times, but the place was bustling compared to any other visit. Excitement crackled in the air as palpable as someone getting their hands on a sheet of Bubble

Wrap. She wasn't sure what was going on, but something had obviously just happened.

"I need to see Detective West," she said as she came to a stop in front of the ornery Officer Reynolds, who always seemed to work the desk when she came in.

"Course you do," he said with a wink that made Lou shudder. But then his face lit up. "Actually, perfect timing. He was saying he needed you to verify something for him. Let me show you to the room he wants you in."

Reynolds led Lou to a room that held bankers' boxes piled in one corner and a large two-way mirror along the opposite wall. It was empty, as was the room on the other side of the glass. In that room, there was a table and two chairs.

"Just wait here. He'll be right in." Reynolds winked at Lou again.

She wrapped her arms around herself. The cool air, while at first a pleasant reprieve from the stuffy summer weather, now felt too cold as she stood alone in the room. Just as she was about to leave to find Easton, the door to the interrogation room on the other side of the mirror opened.

A young man walked in, followed by Easton. Lou gasped, and then immediately hoped the room she was in was soundproof. The person who sat down across from the detective wore a black hooded sweatshirt. He was probably in his twenties, with dark hair, pudgy cheeks, and a slight build. He was a little taller than Lou, but not much.

She didn't even need to see his shoes to know this was the person she'd seen fleeing the site of Ron's murder the other day. There wasn't a doubt in her mind.

Easton cleared his throat.

The young man glanced up, hopeful. He repositioned his hands from where they'd been wringing in front of him and moved to rub them on his jeans, like he was getting rid of sweat.

"Please state your name," Easton said.

"Aiden Foreman."

"Are you related to David Foreman, who used to work at the Tinsdale steel mill?" Easton asked.

Lou's whole body tingled. This had to be it. Easton had found Ronald's killer. Just as soon as it had come, the excitement left Lou to be replaced with sadness. This poor young man. He had his whole life ahead of him, but he'd let anger and revenge change everything.

Aiden's jaw clenched tight. "I was one when my dad died in the accident." His words were quiet but trembled with emotion.

Easton's voice didn't soften like Lou's heart did at hearing that. "Mr. Foreman, we have an eyewitness who saw someone fitting your description at the scene of the murder of Ronald Rossback on Friday evening at six o'clock." Lou could only see the back of Easton's head from where she stood, but she could picture his face pulling into a tight, unamused frown.

Aiden groaned, leaning forward. "I deliver Mr. Rossback's groceries."

"I asked around at the grocery store," Easton said in a *nice try* tone. "They told me they don't have anyone who delivers to Ron's address. You don't even work there."

Aiden rolled his eyes. "I don't tell them I'm buying them for Ron. They probably wouldn't sell them to me if they knew." The kid paused. "Look, he leaves the back door unlocked when he knows I'm coming. Why would he do that if I was a murderer?"

"Why would you run if you weren't?" Easton crossed his arms.

Aiden's expression fell. "I was scared. I didn't see him at first, because I had my hands full with two bags of groceries."

Aiden gulped and squeezed his eyes shut for a second. "I tripped on his body." He shivered. "I dropped the bags on the counter when I heard a knock on the front door. Then some lady was running around the side of the house and saw me. I freaked. Got out of there. You said it yourself: because of what happened to my dad, everyone assumes I wanted Ron dead." Aiden shrugged.

Easton leaned forward. "So you didn't go upstairs at all?" When Aiden shook his head, Easton frowned.

Lou did too. If Aiden hadn't been upstairs, who had she seen in the window? She turned her attention back to the interrogation room.

"Even if you didn't want Ron dead, why were you helping the man responsible for your father's death?" Easton asked.

"Haven't you ever heard of forgiveness?" Aiden scoffed. When he saw Easton wasn't buying it, he added, "I was furious for a long time, but I've been going to therapy, and my counselor mentioned that forgiving Mr. Rossback might help my anger issues. So I thought I would do something nice for him. I brought him a cake my mom baked, at first, but then we got to talking, and I saw he needed help, so I started delivering his groceries once a week."

"How long have you been delivering Mr. Rossback's groceries?" Easton asked.

Aiden wrinkled his nose. "About two years."

"How did he pay you?" Easton asked. "Are there checks in your account to prove you're telling the truth?"

"No. He always paid me cash under the table." At that statement, Aiden's cheeks blushed a bright red. "Oh man. Is that illegal to admit?"

Easton pressed a knuckle to his temple like he felt a headache coming.

"You can ask Candice, at the grocery store, though. She'll

tell you I come in every Friday to get the same things: spaghetti, macaroni and cheese, and canned soups."

Easton made a note to himself, probably to do just that.

"Did Mr. Rossback and you talk at all when you dropped off his groceries?" Easton asked.

Aiden nodded. "We talked a lot." Aiden cleared his throat nervously.

"About ...?" Easton leaned forward, just an inch or two.

"My life. He always wanted to know how I was doing. He really cared. He also talked a lot about his regrets, the things he wished he'd done differently." Aiden's brown eyes met Easton's. "He felt awful about what happened. Said he wished he could've died instead. I know everyone hated him—I did too for most of my life—but it's not what it seems. He wasn't a bad person."

That matched with what Lou had learned about Ron from Jeff Jeffries.

"So you're saying you just arrived at the house minutes before you ran away?" Easton asked, his tone lightening as he realized Aiden was looking less and less like the killer.

"Yeah." Aiden dug in his pocket and pulled out his wallet. "I was at the grocery store until"—he peered at a receipt and said —"five forty-three." After passing the receipt over to Easton, Aiden put his wallet back in his pocket. "Does that clear me?"

Easton swallowed. "Well, I'm going to have to check this out with the people at the grocery store." He coughed. "But, yeah. This helps. Did he mention anyone who might want to hurt him?" Easton asked. "Anyone that had been threatening him lately?"

Lou didn't miss the fact that Easton said *lately*. She was sure Ronald got a bucketful of threats back when the accident and closure were fresh in people's memories.

"No," Aiden said, "but he was kind of losing it, if I'm being honest. In the weeks leading up to"—Aiden swallowed—"Friday, he'd become obsessed with the idea that his house was haunted. Said he heard the ghost moving through the walls. Even said he could smell her perfume." Aiden snorted. "I thought he was crazy. I mean, it's a creaky house. Though I smelled the perfume he was talking about right before I found him. It was like dusty roses."

Lou thought back to the creaking sound she'd heard while she'd waited for Easton and the other cops to show up. She'd assumed that was just normal old, dilapidated house sounds, like Aiden did. But if Ron had lived in that house for thirty years, as the realty site she'd found reported, and hadn't left it much in the last decade, he would've known all the normal sounds. If the creaks were out of the ordinary, Lou wouldn't have blamed him for jumping to conclusions.

She also pondered the perfume smell Aiden had mentioned. She hadn't smelled anything roselike at all. But it was possible it had diminished by the time she'd walked into the room. Was this ghost responsible for Ronald's death?

Lou almost snorted out a laugh at her silliness. Of course a ghost hadn't killed the man. Ghosts didn't exist. Right? A shiver worked its way down Lou's spine.

Easton sighed. "Okay, Aiden. Anything else you can remember from that day that you think will be helpful in finding Mr. Rossback's killer, since it wasn't you?" Easton asked the last part flatly, letting the kid know that he didn't 100 percent believe him.

Aiden shook his head. "I promise. That's it."

Easton stood and motioned for Aiden to follow him.

Then Lou was alone again. She waited, her mind spinning with the implications of this recent development. If Aiden was there, but wasn't the killer, that meant that Derrick was definitely a suspect. He could've killed Ron and left, leaving his body to be found by Aiden. In that moment, Lou was even more glad her nieces had talked her into coming.

A few minutes later, Easton came into the room where Lou waited. The skin under his eyes was puffy and dark, and his jaw was clenched tight.

"You heard that whole thing?" he asked, his tone flat.

"Yeah." Lou pointed to the front of the station. "Reynolds told me you wanted to have me verify something, and I'd say that was definitely who I saw on Friday running away from Ron's place. Not that you need me, since he admitted to being there."

Easton sighed. "I guess I walked into that one. I told the other officers that if Aiden didn't talk, I would call you in to identify him. I'm not sure if Reynolds is trying to help or ruin my investigation by having you listen in on that." He shook his head. "You know what? It doesn't matter. It's done. We've already been able to verify his alibi with the grocery store, and his story checks out with his mom too. He was there, he ran, but he didn't kill Ronald."

"I think I know who did," Lou said.

"I'm going to be very mad if you tell me it's gotta be ghosts too," Easton said with a humorless chuckle.

"Derrick Hops. He came into my shop today and was saying all sorts of stuff about Ron, like he was glad he's dead. Cassidy told me he's the former steelworkers' union leader and that he has never really gotten over the accident or the mill shut down."

Easton nodded. "I've questioned him already, but he doesn't have an alibi." When Lou raised an eyebrow in question, Easton added, "He said he was at home, alone, so no one can verify that he was."

"I thought he might've been at work." Lou wrinkled her nose. "He told Cassidy he's been working evenings."

Easton frowned. "I didn't realize he'd gotten a job. I'll check into it, but I think what's more likely is that Ron wasn't as much of a recluse as we all thought he was. Maybe the woman had visited before, and he was trying to keep her a secret. I think Aiden gave us something important with that perfume clue. I'd bet whoever wears that perfume is the person who killed Ron."

CHAPTER 13

Lou dragged her feet as she left the police station, heading back to the bookshop. Whereas she'd almost run to the station, her steps were much slower on her return journey.

She should've been elated. They'd eliminated yet another suspect, and Easton had a new lead to follow with the perfume clue Aiden had given him. But something felt off. It seemed like they were missing something; she just couldn't figure out what.

The confusion she was already experiencing only increased as she pulled on the door to the bookshop, and it didn't budge. It was still locked. Her nieces raced forward, flipping the lock and pulling her inside, excitement evident in their rapid movements and bunched postures.

"You were there for a while," Mia said.

"That means Easton must've listened to you." Maddy nodded.

Lou was about to explain everything when a knock came on the door. Willow stood outside, holding a glass container. She waved at them and pointed to the locked door. It was then that Lou remembered she was coming over tonight for dinner and a movie with the girls. Willow had grilled a few steaks and Lou was responsible for the salad portion of the meal. Luckily, she'd already prepped the ingredients that morning, before her day had taken such a confusing turn.

Mia raced over to let Willow inside. "You're just in time. Auntie Lou just got back from the police station. She told Easton about how we think some Derrick guy might've killed Ron."

"Derrick who?" Willow scrunched her forehead together.

"Hops. You know him?" Lou asked.

Willow's eyes grew big. "His kids went through the high school," Willow said. "He had a real temper. Each time grades went out, he'd come in and ream out at least one teacher for not seeing his kid's potential."

Motioning to the apartment upstairs, Lou said, "Keep talking, but let's get dinner ready as we do."

"Good idea. I just pulled these off the grill, so they should be ready to cut anytime now." Willow patted the container as she followed Lou and the girls up the staircase to the apartment.

Lou didn't have space for a grill, nor did she have an outdoor space in which to grill anything, so Willow had volunteered to bring that part of the meal. Lou had prepped a strawberry-and-asparagus salad to feature the grilled meat.

Walking into the apartment, Lou felt a cool breeze flowing through the open windows. The girls must've opened them earlier, and it created a lovely cross breeze through the space. The day had been a nice, cooler break from the high eighties temperatures they'd been experiencing the past few days. Seventy-five seemed like dipping toes into a crystal-clear arctic lake after a long hike. Birds chirped happily in the many trees lining the streets of downtown Button.

Willow got to work cutting up the steak while Lou pulled the prepped salad out of the fridge and the girls set the table.

"So Derrick has a temper," Maddy said, bringing them back to the subject of the investigation.

Willow leaned back on her heels. "Oh boy, does he. Apparently, he was like that all the way from elementary school to high school with his boys. And there are four of them. I feel sorry for their college professors now. I'm sure they're still getting emails from Derrick even though the boys are all technically adults now."

Mia wrinkled her nose. "Mom and Dad never take our side. They're always backing the teacher. Even when Mr. Primball obviously gave me a low grade in algebra because he didn't like that I corrected him on his calculations once."

Maddy snorted. "I think your bad grade had more to do with the fact that you never did any of your homework." She rolled her eyes at her younger sister.

"He always makes me show my work." Mia crossed her arms. "Which is dumb since I can do it all in my head."

Lou beamed as she observed her nieces. Mia had always been incredibly gifted in mathematics, but she knew Joe and Emily had a hard time convincing her to do the assignments her teachers gave her.

"Well, Derrick isn't *ever* on the teacher's side." Willow brought the cut steak over to the table and set a pair of serving tongs next to it. She puffed out her cheeks as if recalling a particularly bad memory. "And he's a stay-at-home dad, so he was always the one to come to conferences instead of his wife."

"He has a job now." Lou brought the salad over, and they all took their seats.

Maddy and Mia nodded when Willow looked up, surprise written in her wide-eyed expression.

"Yeah, he said he's working an evening shift," Mia said. She served herself some salad and topped it with a few slices of steak.

"Which means he probably has an alibi for the time Ron was stabbed." Maddy took the salad bowl from her sister and served herself. She perked up as she passed the bowl to Lou. "Easton can look into that, right?"

Lou served herself. "He said he already did. Derrick was at home, alone."

"Not at work?" Mia asked, wrinkling her forehead.

"Nope." Lou found it just as confusing as her niece seemed to.

"So what took you so long at the police station if Easton already suspected Derrick?" Maddy asked.

"It was weird." Lou shook her head. "I said I had something to tell Easton, and the officer at the desk acted like Easton was expecting me. He put me in a space that looked in on an interrogation room."

Mia sucked in a quick breath, almost choking on a piece of lettuce. She coughed. "You mean one of those places with the two-way mirrors where you can see them, but they can't see you?"

Lou nodded.

"That's so cool," Mia and Maddy said in unison.

Lou didn't have the heart to tell them it really hadn't been. It had seemed more like a storage room than anything else. "But I don't think I was supposed to be there. Easton brought in a kid around George's age. He wore a black hoodie, and I recognized him right away as the person I saw fleeing the scene that day at the mansion. It was Aiden Foreman, the son of a victim of the steel mill accident." Lou paused, but she could feel Mia, Maddy, and Willow's eyes boring into her as they listened, hungry for more. "He admitted to being at the mansion that day. He brought Ron groceries once a week, and he stumbled on to Ron's body."

"Or was the one who stabbed him in the first place," Maddy muttered.

"He has an alibi for the time of death," Lou said, "and he actually seemed to like Ron. Said he first visited because his counselor thought it would be a good idea for him to forgive Ron for what happened to his dad. But once he met him, he figured out that he wasn't so bad."

"So the person you saw running wasn't the person who killed Ron." Willow took a bite of her salad and chewed as she pondered that.

"Then it makes it even more likely that it's Derrick," Maddy said, exasperated.

Shrugging, Lou said, "I think so, too, but Easton wasn't convinced."

Mia and Maddy frowned.

"Why?" Maddy asked.

"Because he was fixated on the fact that Aiden told him he smelled a woman's perfume around Ron's body when he found him," Lou said.

"You didn't smell it?" Willow asked, knowing Lou rarely missed details like that.

Lou shook her head. "It must've dissipated in the air once I arrived. But it's got Easton thinking Ron might've had a woman over, and that's who killed him."

"Once that man gets an idea in his head, he latches on to it," Willow scoffed.

Maddy and Mia bumped shoulders. They pressed their lips together to hide sly smiles.

"What?" Lou asked, putting down her fork.

"Willow totally has a crush on the cute detective guy next door," Maddy said matter-of-factly. "We met him yesterday when we were leaving Willow's, and he totally likes her too."

Willow snorted and scoffed all at once, producing a sputtering sound. "Crush? Oh, no. Mads, you've definitely got that wrong."

"She doesn't." Mia arched an eyebrow.

Lou placed a hand over her mouth to hide her grin. She'd guessed before that Willow had feelings for Easton but didn't want to push her friend, something these teenage girls had no qualms about.

Willow's cheeks grew pink, and her eyes darted around the apartment as if hoping for someone to rescue her. "I ... he's ... there's nothing ... So what if he's cute?" she finally said, exasperated. "So what if he's handsome? He's insufferable!"

Mia laced her fingers together in front of her. "You know what book I just finished reading in English class, Auntie Lou?" Mia asked rhetorically. "*Pride and Prejudice*."

Maddy nodded. "Willow sounds a lot like Lizzy at the beginning, when she was pretending to hate Darcy."

Lou beamed. If she didn't already adore her nieces, that would've done it. Using classic literature to make their point. She was so proud.

Willow sputtered some more. "I'm obviously not going to convince you otherwise," she mumbled. Then her eyes lit up. "Oh, Lou, should we tell them about the trip?" Willow asked Lou, obviously ecstatic about having a different subject to talk about.

The girls leaned forward. "What trip?" Mia asked.

"Do you remember the Free Trips your Uncle Ben and I used to take each year on his birthday?" Lou asked.

"Sure," Maddy said.

"Well," Lou said, "Willow and I were thinking we would keep the tradition going to honor Ben each year around his birthday. And since you were coming to visit so soon after this year, we thought we'd go on the first one with you. You can choose where we go and what we do, but only once we're on the road," Lou explained.

The girls' faces shone with excitement. "When do we get to go?" Mia asked.

Lou rubbed at her chin. "Willow's got a horse show this Saturday, and then Sunday is"—she cleared her throat—"the day, so anytime in between now and then. We could go on Sunday, if you want to be gone for the day, distracted."

Maddy shook her head. Mia mimicked her sister.

"No, I think we should spend Sunday at the bookshop," Maddy said. "Uncle Ben would've liked that."

"We could go tomorrow," Mia suggested.

"Yes, let's go tomorrow." Maddy clapped her hands excitedly.

Lou shrugged and looked at Willow. "That okay with you?"

"Perfect," Willow said.

"You'll need to help us out a little, though." Maddy wrinkled her nose. "We don't know the area or what might be within a day-trip distance."

Lou gestured to Willow. Even though she was getting her bearings more and had grown up just a few hours south of Button, Willow had lived there for a decade.

"Well," Willow said with a smile, cracking her fingers as if she was about to start a long speech, "it depends on how much driving we want to do. If you want a long drive with a shorter activity, we could go up to Bellingham, on the Canadian border, or over to the Cascade Mountain Range. If you want a shorter drive, anywhere in Lakeside County would work for a day trip, though some places are more exciting than others." Willow lifted one shoulder and let it fall. "Tinsdale, as I'm sure you've heard with all the talk around this steel mill and Ronald stuff, is a ghost town. Nothing to do there. Brine is super weird."

"Weird, how?" Maddy asked, interrupting Willow.

"They have no grocery store, but three psychics." Willow snorted. "They try way too hard, but always fall short of us. We have tourists all the time, but they only attract weird ones, like mushroom hunters or groups of people searching for Big Foot in the surrounding forests. Seattle's also available for a day trip, or we could go on a hike." She kept on talking, telling about the different activities around, but Lou could see the girls' eyes sparkling as they looked at each other, and she knew they'd already decided on something.

Lou had a bad feeling that their level of excitement meant she and Willow would regret letting them choose.

CHAPTER 14

Thursday morning, Lou posted a sign on the front door of the bookshop explaining that Whiskers and Words would be closed for the day, and apologized for the inconvenience.

Willow picked them up before eight, so they would be gone before the bookshop was supposed to open. Everything felt right. It promised to be a beautiful bluebird kind of summer day, already in the seventies, without a cloud in the sky. Lou slid her sunglasses up onto her head as she craned her neck to see into the back seat where the girls sat.

"All right, where to?" she asked. "Do we need to stop for coffee or snacks first?"

Mia smiled.

"I don't think so," Maddy said. "We're not going too far, and I think we can get all of those things where we're headed." An excited tremor pulsed through Maddy's words.

Willow narrowed her eyes in question. Lou turned around to look at her nieces.

"We would like to go to Brine, please," Mia said, stifling a smile the whole time.

Lou smirked. So that's why they'd been smirking yesterday.

"Brine?" Willow wrinkled her nose and frowned. "Why would you want to go there?"

Mia giggled.

"Because it sounds awesome," Maddy scoffed. "Three psychics in the same town? And it's named after pickle juice? Yes, please."

"And the streets are all named after pickling things," Willow muttered.

Maddy laughed. "Even better."

"But they have coffee and snacks there, right?" Mia asked.

Willow grumbled a confirmation. Lou pressed her lips together.

"We told them they could choose *anywhere*," Lou reminded her friend.

Willow sighed and pulled out onto Thread Lane, heading for Brine. "And what are we going to do while we're there?" she asked, only slightly grumpily.

Maddy tsked. "Nuh-uh, Willow. This is a Free Trip. We have to decide everything once we get there. We can't make plans."

The girls beamed in the back seat, getting way too much pleasure out of this. Ben used to sport the same goofy grin at the beginning of each Free Trip. His nieces were so much like him. The thought made Lou incredibly happy but also hit her with a pang of sadness.

Unlike Button, with all its overt cuteness, Brine's charm grew on a person. Brine's brick and concrete buildings definitely needed a quick power wash to get back to their former glory. Instead of the cute, bright, multicolored trim dotted through the downtown businesses of Button, the only thing that really held the buildings in Brine together was their collective dinginess.

But it was still cute, in Lou's eyes. The way the girls smiled and oohed, she knew they shared her sentiments about the small town to the east.

And it *really* was small.

While Button housed a couple thousand residents, Willow explained that Brine only had half of that.

"Where do they grocery shop?" Lou asked as they drove north on Gherkin Street.

"They head down to Silver Lake mostly, probably because the people of Button aren't the most welcoming to them." Willow's tone dropped at the end in a way that told Lou she was feeling a little embarrassed about how the people of Button treated their sister town, now that they were here.

"They have a pickle festival?" Mia's eyes were wide as she read the large sign next to the Welcome to Brine sign.

"Aw, we're going to miss it." Maddy snapped her fingers in disappointment, pointing to the date in early August.

Willow laughed. "Don't be too sad. It's mostly them pickling things that should never be pickled and then wondering why people don't want to try them."

The girls giggled again as Willow pulled onto Relish Road. Parking—in Pickle Parking Lot, of course—they got out and crossed the street to grab coffee at Salty Roasters and breakfast at Brine Bakery.

The coffeehouse held a quirky vibe that felt along the same lines as the Bean and Button. They'd obviously spent decades collecting pickle Christmas ornaments, because about a hundred hung from strings suspended in the ceiling, creating a canopy of pickles above their heads as they ordered their drinks. The bakery held the normal fare of breads, muffins, and desserts, but it also offered weird things like pickle scones and pickle-flavored cupcakes. But even the teenagers weren't brave enough to try the pickle cupcakes.

Coffees in hand and non-pickle-flavored muffins disappearing quickly, they walked down Cornichon Road. Lou was about to ask the girls what they wanted to do next when Maddy stopped and sucked in a breath. Mia smiled.

They were staring at a string of five businesses, all next to one another. One was a doughnut shop. Next to it, on the end, was a place called The Briny Beyond: from the neon signs in the windows, it was home to tarot and palm readings as well as gemstones and clothing. On the other side of the doughnut shop, was a tarot reading business and a palm reading business. The last shop on the left was a dry cleaner.

"Can we go get our palms read?" Mia jumped up and down.

"Or our tarot cards pulled?" Maddy added.

"Sure," Lou said, then frowned. "Which place should we go?"

She'd definitely heard of towns having more than one of the same type of business but hadn't ever heard of them all being on the same block.

Willow pointed to The Briny Beyond. "This one has everything, so it seems like the obvious choice."

They crossed the street and entered, a gentle crystal chime tinkling softly as they walked through the front door. Inside, the air didn't just smell of nag champa incense, but it pulsed with the curling, fragrant smoke. Lou breathed it in, loving the smell of incense and reminding herself to pick up some for her apartment.

Crystals and other precious gemstones sat in containers ranging from wooden bowls to large geodes in the shape of serving bowls. Crystals and feathers hung from the ceiling in an artistic fantasy kabob of items. A drum-and-bagpipes-based soundtrack played in the background, and Lou thought she recognized it from the show *Outlander*.

Dream catchers, racks of flowing scarves and long skirts,

and an entire wall of books completed the small room, but there was no one inside. A dark purple tie-dyed curtain hung across the only doorframe in the space, and a set of rickety stairs led up to a little loft area where Lou could just barely glimpse a small table set up and an old couch draped with different colored scarves. The girls had gravitated toward the gemstones and read through what each one stood for, energy-wise.

"Coming!" trilled a voice from behind the curtain.

Willow raised her eyebrows at Lou.

A moment later, a woman swept through the curtain. That wasn't an exaggeration. She swept, arching an arm to move the curtain out of her way, and then letting it hang, arm curved in the air as she spun in a graceful circle. At first, Lou thought the curtain had gotten tangled up around the woman, but her clothing was just made of the same purple tie-dyed silk. She had brown hair that was pulled back, held in place by two decorative chopsticks, and gray hairs frizzed out from her head, creating a shining halo. She had large brown eyes like a deer and blinked them as she took in the group of four.

An enormous smile pulled across her face as she took in Willow and the girls, but when her gaze landed on Lou, her expression dropped into a sorrowful scowl. Before Lou could figure out what was happening, the woman lunged forward and pulled Lou into a gentle hug. It was the exact opposite of a Willow hug, like being lightly surrounded by feathers. Unlike Willow, who always squeezed too tight, this woman almost put no pressure on Lou at all. But even though, at first, Lou found it unsatisfying, after a few seconds, she felt completely encompassed by the woman's sympathy.

As the woman stepped back, Lou asked, "What was that for? I'm sorry, have we met?"

The woman pursed her lips. "Never. You just have the

energy of a person in mourning, and I had a feeling you needed a hug." Holding out a thin hand, the woman said, "My name is Francine."

Lou had sort of been expecting her to say something like Amethyst, Lavender, or Moon Spirit.

"Well, thank you, Francine." Lou smiled wider. She felt the girls step forward to stand next to her.

"You're so right," Mia said with a gasp. "This is our aunt, and she *is* in mourning."

Maddy's mouth hung open. "Our uncle died a year ago this Sunday, and we're all still super sad, our aunt most of all." She gestured to Lou.

Willow hissed out a shush. "You're not supposed to tell her all of that. Isn't she supposed to figure that out on her own?"

Francine cocked her head and studied Willow. "Oh dear. I'm psychic, not a mind reader." She patted Willow's cheek affectionately as if she were a silly child. "I can only read energy and intentions, not tell exactly what happened in the past or what will happen in the future." She winked at the girls. "That stuff's mostly in the movies." Francine let her hand drop from Willow's skin as if it had burned her. She stared at her fingers for a moment. "For example, I can tell that you're holding back from letting yourself have what you've always wanted. You've been burned by love in a way that has made you closed off to the idea, even though you have powerful feelings for another." Francine closed her eyes. "I'm getting a sense that he's very close to you."

Maddy let out a surprised laugh. "Willow!" she screeched out in excitement. "She's totally talking about Easton."

"He lives right next to her," Mia told Francine. "We were just telling her yesterday that she loves him. She wouldn't believe us."

Lou felt torn between completely agreeing with what

Francine and the girls were saying but also hating to see the cornered expression on Willow's face. She had to save her friend. It was what they did for each other. They had the other's back, always.

Lou stepped between Willow and Francine, saying, "Actually, we mostly came in here for the girls, not the two of us." Lou motioned toward the teenagers to move Francine's attention from Willow.

Francine studied her for a moment. "Of course." She turned to Mia and Maddy. "And what brings you in today? No, don't tell me. Let me read your energy." She closed her eyes and held out her hands like there was an invisible glass wall in front of her.

Mia and Maddy held still, glancing at each other, unsure if they were supposed to be doing anything at that moment.

"Hmmm..." Francine's lips pulled into a thin line. "I'm reading a lot of sadness as well, which makes sense, given what you said about your uncle's passing." Francine's eyes popped open, and her hands dropped back down by her sides. "But the overwhelming feeling I'm getting from the both of you is that of curiosity."

The girls looked at each other and then back to Francine.

"And we all know what they say about curiosity?" Francine waited.

"It killed the cat?" Mia guessed.

Francine burst out into laughter. "Oh, that's good. I almost forgot about that one. No, that you should treat your curiosity as the most useful gift you were endowed with, of course."

"Eleanor Roosevelt said that." Lou broke into a wide smile. Ben used to use that quote in his freshman English classes. She'd always loved it.

Francine was officially Lou's favorite person in Brine so far.

From the tense set of Willow's jaw, Lou could tell her best friend didn't agree.

"Should we do palm readings or tarot readings to figure out the answers we seek?" Maddy asked in a hushed tone. She'd officially bought in as well.

Francine shook her head. "Those things will only give you answers about what lies inside your heart and mind already. I get the sense that you seek answers of the physical world beyond what you already understand."

They stared at her, waiting for her to tell them what that meant.

Francine chuckled. "Which means we should probably just chat over some tea and I'll see if any visions come to me."

The girls blinked in surprise.

"Oh, okay," Mia said.

Thirty minutes later, they'd each purchased some stones, a few decorative scarves, a pack of incense for Lou, and four mugs of truth tea.

Situated upstairs, they got comfy on the couch and floor pillows, watching Francine as she settled on the floor in between them. She sipped her own tea, humming an indistinguishable song as she rocked back and forth.

Lou was about to ask how long this would take when Francine coughed out an exhale. "Oh, I'm getting a sense of a place. It's very dusty. The answers you seek lie in a place covered in dust." She waved her hand in the air in front of her as if to get rid of the dust that wasn't in the room.

Maddy and Mia looked over at Lou, wide eyed. Willow rolled her eyes.

"The mansion is probably super dusty," Mia said. "There must be more answers there."

Francine nodded, not opening her eyes. "Yes, there's something very important to do with time. I'm feeling a powerful pull toward that. It's showing up with a capital letter. Very important. Time."

"I wonder if there are any clocks hiding clues in Ronald's house?" Maddy wondered aloud.

Francine's eyes snapped open. Her dewy countenance fell flat, looking drawn and angry. "Ronald?"

"Yes, Ronald Rossback," Lou said. "He was killed a week ago in our town, and we're trying to figure out what happened—who did it."

Francine's kind, airy voice grew angry and tight. "No." She stood abruptly. "You need to leave right now. I will not have anyone speak that man's name in my place of business."

Willow stood, her shoulders set back in the way they always got when she was about to be stubborn. Lou braced herself for Willow to give Francine a piece of her mind.

Mia grabbed Willow's hand, stopping her. The teenager locked eyes with Francine and asked, "Did someone you love get hurt in the accident?"

Francine flinched, her eyes darting away as if she couldn't bear to look at the teenager. "Yes," she said after a moment. "My husband. He hurt his leg, badly." She sniffed. "We were some of the luckier ones, though." She settled back into the chair.

Willow did too. "We're sorry to hear that."

The comment Silas made about Ron's hurtful impact reaching far beyond the families who lost someone in the accident came back to Lou yet again. But this time the thought came with a bout of fear. They needed to be careful. Enemies of Ron's were everywhere, and they'd obviously stumbled upon yet another.

Blinking, as if seeing her customers through fresh eyes, Francine said, "Why are you trying to get inside Ronald's house?"

"We're going to figure out who killed him," Maddy said, crossing her arms over her chest.

A puff of laughter burst out of Francine as if she couldn't contain it. "Oh, dear child. I can tell you exactly who killed Ronald Rossback."

CHAPTER 15

Willow sat back in surprise. Maddy and Mia leaned forward, eager to hear what the psychic would say next.

Lou was still dubious about the claim Francine had just made about Ronald's killer. "Because you're a psychic and you got a vision?" she asked with a frown.

Francine fidgeted with her long, flowing top. "No, but I know someone who talked a big game for years about getting Ronald back for what he put Lakeside County through."

"Who?" Mia asked, the word engulfed in a gasp.

"Our union president," Francine said matter-of-factly. "He was always the only one looking out for the steelworkers, and he swore he would make Ronald pay for what he did, no matter how long it took."

The girls widened their eyes at Lou. Willow's lips parted in surprise. Derrick.

"And you're not worried that telling us that might give us cause to tell the police?" Lou leaned toward Francine.

The psychic shrugged. "The police in this whole county

hated Ron as much as the rest of us. I doubt you'll find anyone who's invested in putting Ron's murderer behind bars."

Lou pondered this. Easton had said that they were moving on from Ron's case, giving him little help, and piling on new cases. Reynolds had let her sit in on an entire interrogation of a suspect, which she guessed she wasn't supposed to have done, from the way Easton had reacted. He'd been upset that the other officers were trying to discredit his case.

"Easton will find the truth," Willow said, standing up. "He's a good detective."

Francine only smiled. "Ah," she said, looking to Mia and then Maddy with a nod. "I see what you're saying now. Yes, this one is definitely in love."

Willow clenched her jaw. Lou stood and asked, "How much do we owe you for the session?"

Francine waved a hand. "Nothing. Please, I didn't give you anything."

Lou thanked her as they left, but Francine was wrong. She'd given them all a lot to think about.

The group of four wandered down the street after leaving The Briny Beyond. Silence settled over them as they each digested what had happened in the shop. Their purchases bumped along in bags at their sides.

"So, Derrick?" Willow said absentmindedly as they walked.

Lou shoved her hands into her jeans pockets. "She seemed pretty sure it was him."

It took Lou and Willow a few feet to realize they were walking alone. They turned to find the teenage girls stopped in the middle of the sidewalk, hips cocked, attitude in their tilted heads.

"That's what you two are focusing on?" Maddy scoffed.

"Not the fact that she told us Willow is in love with Easton?

How is that not the most important?" Mia raised her hands, palms up, in frustration.

Willow's cheeks went red, and Lou stepped forward to save her friend. It didn't matter how much she agreed. She knew Willow needed to go at her own pace.

"Okay, you two. That's enough matchmaking for today." Lou smiled and threw an arm around each of her niece's shoulders, making them laugh as they continued to walk.

They found themselves back where they had parked the car. The lot was next to Pickle Lake.

Whereas Button had many smaller lakes within the town limits, Brine only had one large lake in the shape of a pickle. A jogging path wound around its banks, making for a lovely walk, and plaques along the path gave out pickling facts. They walked it twice before heading back to the car.

"Okay, I have to admit that Brine is kinda fun," Willow said after their walk. "Anything else before we head home? There's a theater, but I think it's a playhouse, not a movie theater, and I doubt there's a show on a Thursday afternoon."

The girls shrugged.

"That's okay. This was fun enough." Mia smiled.

Maddy nodded. "I think I'm ready to go back."

Lou understood the sentiment. Their time at The Briny Beyond had been an emotional drain of sorts. She was more than ready to get back home.

MIA AND MADDY spent Friday with Willow. She had a ton of work to do to get ready for her show with OC the following day, and the girls were more than happy to help. She picked them up outside the bookshop, waving at Lou who stood in the front doorway as they left.

Without her nieces in the shop, Lou settled back into her everyday routines. While she missed their presence—they brought a substantial amount of conversation and laughter—she also loved the quiet of running the place on her own. But she felt plenty of company since they'd checked all the cats yesterday when they'd returned from Brine, and everyone was officially flea free.

It felt right having all the cats in the shop once more. She'd been right about people leaving the Artful Clawdger alone once he wasn't the only cat. The people who weren't so impressed with him simply kept their focus on the other felines. And the ones who had a sympathetic heart for the little guy sought him out.

But there was one cat who was getting the lion's share of attention. Miss Clawvisham was a veritable celebrity. It didn't hurt that her favorite place to nap was in one of the two front windows, fully drenched in morning sunlight.

Customers had been coming in all day just to pet the gorgeous cat they'd seen in the window. So it didn't surprise Lou when a woman came in around lunchtime, asking for an adoption application for the beautiful Rag Doll. Lou beamed, though a little piece of her wished some of the cats who'd been there longer could've been in the spotlight as much as the newcomer.

The woman who filled out the application reminded Lou of Peggy, ironically. She had similar-looking brown hair, looped into a large plastic clip at the nape of her neck. Lou hoped that was a good sign, that the cat would get a second chance with a person who loved her just as much as Peggy seemed to.

Lou explained that she would be in touch once her coworker had a chance to look it over. After a few adoptions, Noah and Lou had decided they should both look over each application before they placed a cat in a new home. Noah often knew the locals and their past with pets better than Lou.

The woman, Jane, hunched in disappointment at first but said she would be back tomorrow. Once Jane had gone, Lou texted Noah.

> Got an application for Miss Clawvisham. Want to stop by this evening or should I scan it to you?

He didn't text back until after lunch, but Fridays were usually his busy day for spays, neuters, and other surgeries.

> No need to scan. I have a break in my surgeries and can swing by. Heading your way now. Be there in five.

A few minutes later, Noah walked through the door. He fixed Lou with his signature dimpled smile and strode over.

"How's your day going?" he asked.

His presence made Lou feel like someone had wrapped a heavy blanket around her shoulders. It was grounding in the most calming way.

"Fine. It seems like it's a lot less hectic than yours." She smiled an apology as he yawned.

Noah smoothed the front of his shirt. "This week has been a little crazy. And Marigold had a big project due today for science camp, so we were up late last night with the finishing touches on her board." He shook his head. "I can't even be mad at her for procrastinating because she sure didn't get that trait from Cass."

"You don't strike me as a procrastinator," Lou said. "You're always jumping to help everyone right when they ask."

"Yeah, helping people is something I enjoy. That I'll do right away. Taxes? Cleaning the gutters? Not so much." He blinked his eyes as if to keep himself awake, then looked around. "Are you alone? I was excited to meet your nieces. I'm sorry I haven't gotten the chance yet. Everyone in town says they're lovely young ladies."

Lou beamed. "They're with Willow having a barn day. They live in Montana, so they're horseback riders as well, and know how to help her prep for a dressage competition tomorrow. Plus, who doesn't love spending time with Willow?"

"Good point," Noah said.

"Maddy, the seventeen-year-old, would love to meet you, actually. She's considering being a veterinarian." Lou handed over the application. "Anyway, the reason you're here."

Noah took the paper from Lou, his eyes already poring over the page. "I'm not surprised she's already getting snatched up. She's just beautiful."

"You should've seen the number of people who came in this morning just because they saw her through the window. She's great for business, but I want her to have a good home more than I need her help with customers." Noticing Noah was frowning at the paper, Lou asked, "Do you know that person? She didn't look familiar to me, but I'm still learning."

Noah inhaled. "I don't know her, but the name seems familiar." Pulling out his phone, Noah typed something and waited. "I'm asking Kathleen. She remembers everything."

Lou smiled. She liked the no-nonsense woman who ran the clinic with Noah. Kathleen was also incredible at remembering information about clients and their pets. Lou used a trick with her authors back when she was an editor. She wrote information about things they'd shared with her on a note card so she could jog her memory before she spoke to them. She knew sometimes when you went months without seeing the person, little details got lost.

Kathleen seemed to know everything, and she didn't use any such note card trick.

Noah's phone vibrated in notification as a text came through. His frown deepened as he read over Kathleen's response. "We have a problem," he said to Lou, pivoting the phone so Lou could read the message from the receptionist.

> Yes, that name is familiar. She's on the do-not-adopt-to list.

"There's such a thing as a do-not-adopt-to list?" Lou's head shot back in surprise.

Noah nodded. "A couple of years ago, we had a problem with a local adoption group. They would adopt up a bunch of animals, and weeks later, we would find them attempting to sell them on Craigslist or other pet sales sites in the city. It's why I've started taking over the adoptions in town mainly. I just lost trust in people."

A warmth moved through Lou at the realization that he'd trusted her right away, letting her help foster and adopt out cats the first week she moved to town.

"That's awful." A sick feeling churned in Lou's stomach. "I'm so glad I waited to have you check this application. Can you imagine if I'd let her adopt Miss Clawvisham today like she wanted to?" Lou shivered.

"Yeah, I think our policy of making people wait a day while we check over their paperwork is a good practice we should continue," Noah said.

"I can't wait until she tries to come back tomorrow." Lou narrowed her eyes. "I'm ready to give her a piece of my mind."

"I doubt you'll see her again," Noah said. "The moment you told her she would have to wait, I'm sure she knew you would look her up."

Lou pressed her lips together. It sounded like she was going to have to be more vigilant than she thought when finding these cats homes.

But before Lou could think about that much more, she got a text from Willow.

S.O.S.

CHAPTER 16

Lou's fingers shook as she pulled out her phone and called her friend. Noah stood by, his features marred with concern.

"What's wrong?" Lou asked, tension creating an edge to her question.

There was a splashing sound in the background. Lou's mind scrolled through the possibilities. Had there been a plumbing issue at Willow's? At least that was better than someone being hurt, like Lou had first worried.

"Hey!" Willow said as she laughed. "I'm holding a phone, you wild child. Don't spray me. I'm talking to your aunt." Giggles danced in the background.

Lou's chin dropped in frustration. This didn't sound like an emergency at all.

"Willow, focus," Lou said into the phone.

"Sorry," Willow said, her voice clearer now, like she was holding the phone correctly this time. "Those nieces of yours are a silly bunch."

Lou rolled her neck back and forth to release the tension

and irritation she was feeling. "They are. Now why did you text me SOS.? What's the emergency?"

"Oh," Willow said, like she'd forgotten. "A buckle on my cinch broke and I need a new one. They have the one I need at a local tack shop, but it isn't open tomorrow, and they close in a couple of hours. I've got a sudsy horse who still needs to be rinsed and braided. Is there any way you can close early, come grab my car, and drive up north to grab it for me?"

Lou's heartbeat relaxed. That was all? A tack malfunction. She could handle that. Her morning had been so busy that closing early didn't sound like a hardship at all.

"Sure," she said. "I'll be right over."

"Thanks!" Willow hung up the call.

Lou shook her head as Noah laughed. "Sounds like everything's okay," he said.

"Just Willow being dramatic, as usual." Lou rolled her eyes. "I'd better get going, though. I've got an errand to run. Thank you for your help." She smiled at him.

Noah walked with her to the front door of the shop. "Anytime. I hope I can meet your nieces before they leave."

"Me too." She locked the door behind them, and they parted ways: Lou heading down toward Willow's house, and Noah walking back to the clinic to finish his busy day.

WHAT WILLOW DIDN'T TELL Lou on the phone was that the tack shop was almost an hour's drive north. But Lou didn't really mind. She put on some music and enjoyed the drive, especially since driving was something she hadn't done regularly for a while.

With the windows down, and the breeze whipping through the car, Lou decided it was time for her to get her own vehicle.

Not only would it be getting cold and rainy in a few months, but Lou liked the freedom it brought. Plus, it reminded her of when she and Ben would take trips out to see their families. They'd always rent a car and thoroughly enjoyed the novelty of it while it was theirs.

Luckily, Willow had called ahead, and the shop was holding the specific piece she needed. Lou knew what a cinch strap was —it was the part that wrapped around the horse's belly to keep the saddle on—but she didn't know what size or type Willow needed from the wall of options hanging in the tack shop. She paid with the cash Willow had given her and was headed back to the car within minutes of arriving.

But as she was climbing back into the car, ready to make the return journey to Button, a vehicle she recognized passed by her on the main road.

It was a lifted maroon diesel truck.

Derrick Hops. What was he doing so far north?

Starting the car, Lou pulled out of the tack shop's parking lot and followed the truck. Checking the time, she realized it was just after three thirty.

Was this about the time when an evening shift might begin? she wondered.

It was a Friday. Questions about Derrick's job had plagued Lou ever since the discrepancy between what he'd told Cassidy and Easton. Francine's confidence that he was the one who'd killed Ron had only increased Lou's interest in the former union president.

After about ten minutes, Lou was beginning to wonder if the man was driving all the way up to Canada. She slowed to turn around when Derrick turned left. Lou followed but stayed back at a farther distance as they drove into a business park. The streets were lined with oak trees and were large enough for semitrucks to move about comfortably. Enormous warehouses sat on either side of Lou. Up ahead, Derrick took a left into one of the parking lots. Lou drove straight, though she slowed down considerably. He didn't park in the lot, however, instead pulling around behind the building.

But she didn't see him anywhere. That didn't mean he wasn't inside. He could've easily parked in the back and entered through a rear door.

Lou took a right into the parking lot and pulled into a spot facing away from the business Derrick had parked behind. It was a business called Dante's. Squinting, she tried to see Derrick inside. What if he was just going in for an appointment? Why had he parked in the back, then? It was hard to see through the rearview mirror, but she didn't want to risk facing the business and being too obvious that she was spying. Her window was down, and she tried using the side mirror to get a different angle, but she still couldn't see him.

What she really needed to do was go inside. If Derrick wasn't anywhere to be seen, she could ask if he was working last Friday. If he was inside, she could pretend to be there to ask about the business. But what did Dante's sell or do? From what Lou could see, it was just a regular office building. She needed to find out more about the business before blindly walking inside.

She was about to look it up on her phone when the time caught her eye on the dashboard of the car. Lou's head shot back in surprise at how late it had gotten. It was almost four o'clock. Marigold usually came in on Friday evenings to brush the cats. With her errand for Willow, Lou had completely forgotten. And while she'd seen Noah earlier, and he knew about her closing early, Marigold was usually with her mom on Fridays because of her dad's busy surgery schedule. Lou pulled out her phone and called Cassidy.

"Hey, what's up?" Cassidy answered.

144

"I'm running some errands for Willow, and I won't be back in time to meet Marigold at the shop. Would you let her know I need to take a rain check for this week too?" Lou asked.

"Sure," Cassidy said. "I actually came early to catch the end of practice, so that works perfectly. We'll just head home." Now Lou could clearly hear the sound of softball practice in the background.

"Great." She studied the building behind her through her mirror. "Hey," she said, figuring Cassidy would be the right person to ask. She knew Derrick, so she probably knew what his business did. "What do you know about the place Derrick works?" Lou asked.

Cassidy paused as if remembering the other day. "Considering that it shocked me to hear he had a job, nothing. Last I'd heard, he was staying home with the boys."

"Oh." Lou's hope deflated. "I see. I think I just saw him walk into a place called Dante's up north. Could he work there?"

Cassidy snorted. "Uh, no way. Derrick wouldn't be caught dead there."

"Why?" Lou studied the front of the inconspicuous office building, wondering if it was a front for something awful.

"Dante's is a cut-rate shipping company," Cassidy explained. "They're infamously against unions. It's a big corporation that constantly puts profits ahead of workers. It's basically everything Derrick hates in this world."

Lou clicked her tongue. "Well, I think I just saw him walk inside. And he was wearing a tie." She craned her neck and peered at the rearview. When she couldn't find him in that mirror, she moved to check the side mirror.

Lou jumped as she realized someone was standing directly outside of her open driver's side window. To her horror, it was unmistakably the hulking frame of Derrick Hops. He stood with his arms crossed, a scowl on his face.

"What are you doing?" he asked.

Lou let out a surprised yelp.

"Lou, is everything okay?" Cassidy asked on the other end of the call.

"I think so. Sorry, Cassidy. I've got to go. Derrick Hops is standing next to my car." Lou said the words slowly so Cassidy might understand that she could be in danger. "I'm going to hang up now," Lou said even though she had every intention of staying on the line, and she hoped Cassidy would too.

Pretending to end the call, Lou set the phone in her lap so Cassidy could still hear. She didn't dare check the screen to see if Cassidy was still connected, but she hoped she was.

"Hi, Derrick. It's Lou. I own the bookshop in Button, remember?" She wondered how fast she could start Willow's car and zoom out of the parking spot. Derrick was a big man. Could he stop her car? She jabbed a thumb behind her. "Do you work here?"

Instead of answering her question, he glanced at her phone. "Why were you talking to Cassidy French? What did you tell her?"

"Oh." Lou snorted out a fake laugh. "It's the funniest thing. I was on the phone with Cassidy about something else. Then I saw your truck, and I was like, hey I think I just saw Derrick. Does he work at Dante's?" Lou pressed her lips together. She left out the part about Cassidy mentioning he wouldn't be caught dead working there.

The big man raked his hand through his hair. "So she knows. That means everyone else will know soon." His face crumpled together like he might cry.

"Hey," Lou said, softening. "Everyone will know what?" Lou braced herself to hear a confession of murder. Would he break and tell her what he'd done?

"That I've sold out," Derrick said. "I held out for so long, trying to find a job that helped me stand up for the little guy, like my union position. It turns out there were a lot of places that don't want an ex-union president with anger management issues. I burned a lot of local bridges after the mill went under. And I was content doing the stay-at-home dad thing for a long time, but now the boys are in college and it's expensive. I needed a job. And this one paid well."

Now Lou wished she actually hadn't kept Cassidy on the phone.

"So this is where you work?" Lou asked, adding in, "Monday through Friday?"

"Four to midnight," he said.

Lou wrinkled her forehead. "And you were too embarrassed to tell anyone locally that you had this job?"

"Yes." He slapped his palm against his forehead and let out a groan.

"Lou." The sound came from Lou's lap. "Lou, are you there?" Cassidy was still on the line.

Both Lou and Derrick looked down at the phone. Lou cringed. She mouthed the word "sorry" at Derrick before picking up the phone. "Hey, Cass. I'm here," Lou said.

"Would you hand the phone over to Derrick?" Cassidy asked.

Lou offered the big man her phone. His face darkened, but he took it. The phone looked tiny against his large hand.

"Hello?" he asked, his voice breaking around the word. His mouth dipped into a frown. "Hi, Cassidy. I know, I'm sorry I didn't say anything before." He nodded. "I do. Thank you." A reluctant smile pulled at his lips. "Okay, you take care too." He hung up the call and handed the phone back to Lou.

Lou gripped her phone. She wanted to ask what Cassidy had said but didn't want to pry, having already outed the man's secret with her nosiness.

His body language had changed, though. He was no longer tensed as if a cord had been pulled too tight in his shoulders. His mouth tipped up at one side. "She told me I should never be ashamed that I'm trying to provide for my family. She said everyone in town still loves me and appreciates everything I did for them." He lifted a large shoulder and let it drop.

"Good." Lou smiled. "Look, Derrick, I'm so sorry for following you like this. It's just, I thought you wanted revenge so badly on Ronald and ..." She stopped, not really wanting to voice her suspicions aloud.

"You thought I was the one who stabbed him." Derrick inhaled, his nostrils flaring with the motion. "Yeah, I think many people did. I can't blame them. I threatened to enough times that I knew it would come back on me. And even though I had a perfectly good alibi, I've been telling people I was home, alone. I even lied to the police to keep this a secret. But, no, it wasn't me."

Lou nodded. "I can see that now. You know, lying to the police is grounds for arrest, right?"

Derrick raked a hand through his short-cropped hair. "I know. I'll explain everything to Easton and take the consequences. It was stupid of me to lie. I thought I could keep up the ruse a little longer."

"So you were definitely here last Friday?" Lou asked, just to make sure.

He bobbed his massive head. "I'll get my coworkers to vouch for me with Easton, and I'll come clean about lying about my last alibi."

Glancing at the clock, Lou said, "Well, I'd better get home. Sorry, Derrick."

He puffed out his cheeks. "Nah, don't worry about it. It's time I stopped lying about what I do. Keeping it a secret has really been eating me alive." He held up a hand in a wave and walked back to the building.

Lou started the car and headed for Button, excitement rushing through her at the realization that she'd just cleared another suspect. But the good feeling that came with knowing Derrick hadn't been the one to stab Ronald Rossback was over-shadowed by the terrifying realization that without him as a suspect, she had no more leads.

And while Francine the psychic had obviously been wrong about Derrick being the one to kill Ronald, it seemed she had one thing spot on: Ronald's killer might very well get away with their crime.

CHAPTER 17

Once Lou was on the road home, she called Willow.

"You'll never believe what just happened to me," she said when Willow answered.

"What?" Willow's voice turned low and serious.

Lou was still unable to believe it herself. "Let's just say that Derrick Hops is not the killer. I'll explain everything when I get back, though. I want to tell the girls at the same time."

"Well, we're just finishing up here. Do you want to meet us at the pizza place for dinner?" Willow suggested.

Hunger clawed at Lou's stomach, reminding her she'd barely eaten anything for lunch. "Yes, that sounds perfect. I'll be there as soon as I can. I'm still probably forty-five minutes away."

"Okay. See you soon! We'll use the time to get ourselves cleaned up," Willow said, hanging up.

For the rest of the drive back to Button, Lou tried playing music and feeling the breeze, but nothing felt as good as it had on the way there. Ronald's murder case had her thoughts reeling.

Where did they search next? Heather Foreman, Aiden's

mother? But Easton hadn't even mentioned her, which had caused Lou to assume the woman had a good alibi. Could she have been wrong?

Lou wondered if she should take a closer look into Jessie and Chance, the two men she'd written off because they either didn't have family close by, or at all. Maybe there was someone close to them who hadn't been mentioned in the article.

The other, more intimidating option, was that someone who'd either been injured or angered because they'd lost their job could be to blame. As Francine had proven, the impact of the accident and the shutdown rippled through the entire county, not just the town of Tinsdale. If that were the case, Lou shuddered as she thought of the long list of suspects.

Lou drove to Willow's and parked, letting her thoughts settle as the engine ticked and cooled. She needed to get her mind straight, especially if she was going to be present for Willow and her nieces. She wanted to hear all about their fun day getting ready for the horse show.

Grabbing her phone from the seat next to her, Lou realized she'd missed a text message from Willow about twenty minutes ago.

> Got ready faster than I thought. We're starving! We're going to head over early, grab a table, and order. I'll make sure we get your favorite.

Lou inspected the house in front of her. Fatigue settled over her. She could've just driven straight to the pizza place. She sighed. Oh well. She would just walk there and meet them. After locking up Willow's car and stuffing the keys into her purse, she walked down the street toward Slice o' Button.

As it always did, the Rossback mansion caught her eye as she passed by. She came to a stop on the sidewalk in front of it, staring as her mind filled with questions. What had really happened on Friday? What secrets did the mansion hold?

Movement in a second-story window stopped Lou, making her feel like she was experiencing déjà vu. Her heartbeat ratcheted higher. It was just like the day of Ronald's murder when she was sure she'd seen someone in that same window.

She pulled out her phone, squinting at the house, hoping to see something again.

"Hello?" Easton answered on the second ring.

"I think I just saw someone inside the Rossback mansion, Easton. They were peering out a second-story window, just like I saw last Friday when Ronald was killed." She raced through the explanation as her gaze flicked over each window, searching for another glimpse of the face.

"Okay, I'm on my way. Lou, I need you to get somewhere safe, though. Don't stay there." Rustling in the background told Lou he was on the move.

She nodded. "I'm supposed to meet Willow and my nieces at the pizza place, so I'll head there."

"Good. I'll let you know what we find," Easton said, then hung up.

Lou glanced back at the mansion one last time, then scurried away. Slice o' Button was right next to the police station, and as she passed by, she saw Easton and another two officers donning vests and getting themselves ready to search the mansion. She waved through the window, and Easton waved back. She was glad to see they were taking it seriously.

Inside the pizza place, she located Willow and the girls. Two pizzas had just arrived at the table.

"Just in time," Willow said, motioning to a barbecue chicken pizza, Lou's favorite.

She practically collapsed onto the seat next to her friend. "Thank you."

"So tell us what happened with Derrick," Willow said after swallowing her first bite of pizza.

The girls nodded, chewing their own mouthfuls.

Lou cleared her throat. "Well, first I need to put my phone on the table here so I can see if Easton calls me back. I saw someone inside the mansion on my walk here."

Willow set down the slice of pizza she was bringing toward her mouth, about to take another bite. "What?"

"He's going to check it out now," Lou said.

Circling her hands, Willow said, "Okay, well, fill us in on the Derrick stuff in the meantime."

Lou did, and she was just getting to the part where Derrick was standing outside the open car window, when her phone rang. It was Easton. Lou held out a hand to quiet the table before picking up.

"Hey," she said, trying to keep her voice calm.

"Nothing," Easton said, sounding as disappointed as Lou felt hearing the word. "I thought for a moment there was, but it was just a creaking sound. I can see why Ronald was going crazy. This house plays tricks on you." Easton's voice sounded light, but there was an edge to it. He'd wanted to catch the person inside.

"That's weird. I could've sworn ... Well, thanks for checking." She hung up the call and relayed the information to her table. "They didn't find anyone."

Lou wasn't sure if she was elated or disappointed. Easton's comment about the ghosts Ron had been convinced he saw, heard, and smelled, came to mind. She wondered if she was falling into the same patterns as the reclusive old man.

"Okay, but finish your story about Derrick," Maddy said, her eyes wide.

"Right." Lou told them the rest of what happened with Derrick Hops, and how she knew it hadn't been him.

The girls devoured their slices of pizza as they listened.

"So Francine was wrong about that," Willow scoffed.

"But not about the fact that we need to get inside." Maddy frowned.

Lou blinked at her niece for a moment. "Inside where?"

"The mansion," Mia scoffed as if it was totally obvious.

"Why are we going inside the mansion?" Lou asked.

"Francine said." Maddy moved her head forward, like she was worried about her aunt if she'd already forgotten that encounter. "She said we would find the answers we seek in a dusty place."

Mia nodded. "There aren't any other suspects linked to the accident that we know of, which means there might be clues inside the house."

Lou placed her hands on the table. The embarrassment of making the police search the house for nothing, yet again, was still fresh. "Girls, I think maybe it's time we let the mansion go. We just need to drop it. We have a big, hard day coming up this weekend, and I think I've been focusing on this case to distract myself from dealing with those feelings. It's obviously affecting my concept of reality, and I think you two have been doing the same."

The girls frowned but dropped the subject. Maddy brought up the show tomorrow, and they made their plans. She and Mia would go over with Willow in the morning to get OC checked in and claim a good spot in the spectator seating. They could watch the morning classes, which included hunt-seat equitation and jumping. Then Lou would come out after lunch, since Willow's dressage classes weren't scheduled until the afternoon. That way, Lou could keep the bookshop open for the morning.

Their table was abuzz with excitement about the show.

Everyone seemed to have moved on from the mansion just like Lou had asked them to.

Everyone except Lou.

Her thoughts weren't as compliant. Something Mia said had her thinking. There weren't any other suspects if the motive was Ron's involvement in the steel mill accident. But what if that wasn't it? What if the killer was really there to rob the place, like Easton and the other officers had thought, when they'd first arrived on the scene? It would explain why a person would go back after Ron was already dead.

Even though Easton and the officers hadn't found a person today when they checked the house, that didn't mean it had been empty. The person fled after seeing Lou, before Easton arrived. Come to think of it, the same thing could've happened the day Lou found Ronald's body. She'd seen a person upstairs, and if it hadn't been Aiden—and it obviously wasn't Ron—they had to have gotten out of the house before the police arrived.

Which meant that Maddy, Mia, and Francine, the psychic, all were right. Lou needed to get inside that mansion.

She made a mental note to call Cassidy tomorrow but, as they were leaving after dinner, saw that she didn't need to because Cassidy and Marigold were sitting at a table near the exit.

Willow, Maddy, and Mia waved, but continued outside, waiting for Lou in front of the restaurant. The sun was setting, and it threw gorgeous pinks and oranges along the sky behind them. Lou held up a finger, letting them know she'd be out in a minute, before turning back to Cassidy and Marigold.

"Sorry," Lou said to Marigold. "I was out of town this evening."

"That's okay," Marigold said with a sweet smile.

"Marigold, why don't you go chat with Lou's nieces outside for a second?" Cassidy asked, shooing her daughter outside.

Once the door had closed, she widened her eyes at Lou. "That was pretty crazy today with Derrick."

Lou let out a quick laugh. "Tell me about it. I know you've known the guy your whole life, but I was a little scared there when I saw him standing next to the car."

Cassidy put a hand on her chest. "I have to say, I was a little too. It's why I stayed on the line and listened. But I'm glad everything worked out okay."

"Me too." Lou puffed out her cheeks. She glanced up at the foursome outside and then looked back at Cassidy. Lou narrowed her eyes. "Cassidy, if I wanted to get inside the Rossback mansion, is there a way that could happen?" Lou coughed. "You know, legally?"

Cassidy smiled. "Oh, so you'd like to look at the property? I'd be happy to do a showing with you."

Lou shook her head. "I'm not interested in buying. I just have a few questions I need answered. I think there might be something inside that has to do with why Ronald was killed. Do you know if there's anything valuable in the house?"

"If you want to know about what's inside there or anything valuable, you'll need to talk to Smitty. He'll know the most about what things might be inside or what they're worth," Cassidy said, motioning toward the antique store and mentioning the talkative old man who owned it. "If you're just hoping to get inside, I can do a showing for you, no pressure to buy." Cassidy said the last sentence slow and deliberate, holding eye contact with Lou.

"Oh," Lou said, dragging out the word as she understood Cassidy's meaning. "Yes, I would love that. When can you fit me into your schedule?"

Cassidy pulled out her phone to check her calendar. But before she could answer, Marigold came rushing inside.

"Mom, can I go to a horse show tomorrow with Willow and

Lou's nieces?" Her big brown eyes were even bigger than normal as she pleaded with her mother.

Cassidy turned to Lou. "Are you going to this?"

Lou nodded. "But not until after lunch. Willow's dressage competition isn't until closer to two. I'm going to drive her car later since they'll be taking her truck, which pulls her horse trailer. Marigold can go with Willow and the girls in the morning if she wants to get the full effect. They'll just be watching the other classes and getting Willow set up."

Marigold curled her fingers into tight fists as she waited for her mother's answer.

Cassidy laughed. "Okay. That should work."

Marigold punched the air. "Yes! Thank you, Mom."

"Go find out what time I need to have you at Willow's tomorrow." Cassidy tapped a finger on Marigold's back, and the girl was back out the door. Cassidy turned to Lou. "Well, how about we do a showing tomorrow? I could do something around lunchtime after you close the shop, and then I could drive us both to Willow's show. Save you the extra trip. As long as you can get a ride back with Willow. Does that work for you?"

"That would be perfect," Lou said. "Thanks! See you tomorrow at noon?"

"See you then," Cassidy said as Marigold returned, parroting the time Willow had given her.

The girls and Willow had hit a new level of enthusiasm when Lou walked out to join them. Marigold's excitement seemed to have rubbed off on them. Lou highly doubted there would be much sleeping in either household tonight.

They parted ways with Willow at the roundabout, taking a right toward the bookshop as Willow walked left to her home. Lou glanced over at the antique shop a block down, wondering if Smitty was there late. Cassidy's comment that he would know if there was anything valuable in the house made her itch to speak with him. But the lights in the antique shop were off. It looked like, for once, Smitty had actually gone home on time. Lou's questions would have to wait.

That was okay. Lou wrapped an arm around each of her niece's shoulders, and they walked home to spend a cozy evening with the cats.

CHAPTER 18

"Auntie Lou, is everything okay?" Mia put a hand on her hip and frowned at Lou the next morning.

Mia and Maddy were just about to leave for Willow's, but they stood at the front door of the bookshop, arms crossed, as Lou picked up the books she'd just knocked over. Their concern was warranted. It was the third time she'd knocked over that same stack of books that morning, and she hadn't even opened to customers yet.

"Absolutely. I'm just distracted." She waved a dismissive hand, hoping to quell her nieces' worries.

It wasn't a lie. Lou had been distracted since dinner last night. She knew her nieces would jump to the conclusion that she was having a difficult time with the looming anniversary tomorrow. Even though Ben was on her mind—even more than usual—it was the murder case and what she might find in the mansion that had hogged her thoughts so much that she'd gotten very little sleep.

"We can stay and help you this morning if you need us," Maddy said, eyeing the books as Lou restacked them.

Plastering on a smile, Lou said, "No. Don't be silly. Go ahead. Cassidy and I will meet you at the show. Have the best time, and be a good support for Willow."

The girls warily observed Lou for another second or two, but they finally headed out the front door and down the street.

Finally alone, Lou closed her eyes and placed her palm on her forehead, hoping to center herself. Saturday morning was a busy time for the bookshop, so she needed to get it together. When she opened her eyes, she pulled in a deep breath and went to unlock the front door. The day was going to come, whether or not she was ready.

Lou's focus improved throughout the morning, especially after a large mug of coffee, which was great since the bookshop was packed for the first few hours. At one point, she even checked the maximum occupancy rating near the front door just to make sure they weren't breaking any safety laws. It was *that* packed.

The cats were the stars. Even the Artful Clawdger was getting some love. In fact, one woman in particular seemed to be absolutely smitten with the tortoiseshell cat. Lou shouldn't have been surprised when the same woman with bright red, curly hair came up to the register with a big smile and asked, "Could I get paperwork to fill out for an adoption?"

Lou's eyes went wide as they flicked to the folder of applications by her computer. "Oh, sure. Which one are you interested in?"

"The Artful Clawdger. He's so sweet." The red-haired woman beamed.

And even though Lou completely agreed with her, and had been hoping someone would show the poor, scraggly kitten some love, her last adoption memory was the woman who'd tried to take Miss Clawvisham. The reminder of that woman's ill intentions with the cat sat in her stomach like a sour lump, and she couldn't seem to get excited.

There was too much doubt surrounding this transaction. No one else had really shown him any attention, and those who did seemed to pity him, not want to take him home. How could this not be a scam?

"Sure." Lou fought to create a smile with her lips. "Here's the application. We have a day waiting period so my adoption partner can look over everything. If you want to fill it out, you can leave it with me." Was it just Lou, or did her voice sound super flat and untrusting?

It wasn't just Lou. The woman smirked uncomfortably and took the application, moving to the table where Sapphire lay asleep on a stack of books to fill it out. The red-haired woman took an exceedingly long time to fill out the application, and that only increased the amount of skepticism inside Lou. Still, she texted Noah that there was an application he would need to check over, that it seemed suspicious, and she figured they would go from there.

Around eleven, there was a break in customers that Lou took advantage of. She closed the shop, including a handwritten sign in the window that explained the reason, and urged people to check out the summer classic horse show at the Silver Lake fairgrounds. Because she'd closed a little earlier than she'd expected to, Lou had some time to kill. And while she locked up the bookshop and thought about using that extra time to grab something for lunch, her attention caught on the antique shop a few blocks down the street. Smitty had been closed last night when Cassidy had mentioned asking him about the Rossback mansion, but he was surely open on a Saturday afternoon.

She made her way down the street, savoring the warm

sunlight as it shone down, causing everything to seem shiny and happy. A smile spread on Lou's face as she saw the Open sign hanging in the antique shop window. She entered the dusty, crowded paradise that was Button Antiques. The musty smell of old furniture contrasted with the bright glint of the various cut-glass bowls Smitty had on display at the front of the shop.

"Louisa, how can I help you today?" the old man asked.

He wore his usual uniform of jeans that appeared to be older than Lou, a cracked leather jacket, a blue button-up shirt underneath, and a baseball hat that announced his status as a war veteran.

"Hey, Smitty. Cassidy said I should come chat with you." Lou found it difficult to keep her gaze on the man in front of her. There were so many wonderful treasures in the shop, and she longed to take them all in. Blinking and renewing her focus, she looked back toward Smitty. "I'm interested in the Rossback mansion."

"Looking to buy it?" Smitty asked. He pulled the worn veteran's baseball cap off his head and resettled it as if it had been off just a millimeter.

"No," Lou said. "Honestly, I have a hunch that there's something worth a lot of money in there, that it could be why Ronald was killed. Do you know much about the kinds of antique pieces in the house?"

Smitty's shoulders pushed back as he stood up straighter. "I know a fair amount. When the last family sold the place to Ronald, I bought a fair amount of the furniture, anything Ron didn't want to purchase off them besides a few pieces that had sentimental value to the family."

"And was there anything worth a lot of money? Anything someone might kill for?" Lou asked, leaning against the glass case in between them, filled with old jewelry.

Smitty frowned, studying the ceiling as he thought. "They sold me some marvelous pieces, which makes me sure some of the furniture in there still is made of the same quality. Though, I wouldn't count on it being maintained like the pieces I got from them. Ronald wasn't known for keeping up with maintenance." Smitty rubbed a hand over the gray stubble on his chin. "Let me check through my records."

Lou expected him to turn to the computer he kept on the register counter. Instead, he ducked below the counter and muttered to himself as he searched. Moments later, he reappeared, holding a white three-ring binder.

"Here we go," he said, plucking a pair of reading glasses off the counter and settling them onto his large red nose.

He flipped through pages of notes, some including printed pictures of furniture or collectibles. Pausing, he flipped back two pages, squinting as he reread a certain page more closely than he had the first time through. Just as Lou was about to give up, Smitty inhaled sharply.

"Yes, here's something ..." He tapped the page with a stubby finger. "I remember this now."

Lou leaned forward. The page was an obvious copy of a letter.

"One of the old desks that they sold to me hadn't been cleaned out all the way. There were a few papers left in one drawer, stuck in the back. I looked them over to see if I needed to worry about returning them to the family, which I did, after making copies for myself. One page was a letter from an English pocket-watchmaker to the family's great-grandfather. Apparently he saved the watchmaker's life in World War I, and in thanks, the watchmaker created a custom timepiece for the man." Smitty's milky blue eyes lit up. "From the description of the watch in the letter, I was particularly excited to lay my eyes on the piece. It featured thirty-seven jewels, a split chronograph, and a perpetual calendar that adjusted for leap years."

Lou let out a low whistle. "All of that in the early nineteen hundreds? I bet it was a sight to behold."

Smitty nodded. "Well, I can only guess. I never saw it. When I brought the paper back to them, the daughter said they hadn't been able to locate the pocket watch in any of her mom's belongings. She hoped it was packed away in a box somewhere, but she feared it was lost."

"Lost?" Lou gasped. "How much do you think it would be worth?"

He pushed his lips forward. "I'd say at least a million, if not more."

"That seems like something worth going back to look for." Lou clenched her fingers into fists. "Maybe the daughter came back years later to look for it again?" she asked.

"Could be. Her name was ... Olivia Duncan." Smitty read the handwritten notes he'd taken at the bottom of the photocopy.

Pulling out her phone, Lou searched for an Olivia Duncan in Button, Washington. An obituary report pulled up for a Rose Duncan from thirty years ago, survived by her daughter, Olivia Duncan, and six grandchildren. Lou showed Smitty.

"Yeah, that's it. Rose was the one who owned the mansion before Ronald. She left the place to her only daughter, Olivia, but the woman already had her own house in Kirk and didn't want to have to take care of such a large place, so she sold it off." Smitty spoke faster as the details from all those years ago came back to him.

Revising her search to Kirk, Washington, instead of Button, Lou waited for the results to populate. Excitement built inside Lou as she waited. If she could talk to Olivia, she might figure out who else knew about the pocket watch.

Lou's hopes were dashed when the first result that came up

was for Olivia's obituary. Clicking on it, Lou said, "She died a couple of months ago."

Smitty clicked his tongue. "That's a shame." But he squinted and pointed to the next paragraph on the screen. "She had six kids, though. Maybe one of them is searching for it now that their mother is gone."

Lou pressed her lips into a thin line. "Could be." She checked her watch and saw it was about time for her to meet Cassidy at the Rossback mansion. "I'd better get going." Lou paused. "What would that pocket watch look like? If someone was searching for it today?" she asked.

Smitty raised his eyebrows and wrinkled his forehead. "Something that valuable? I'd say it would come inside a wooden box." He made a square with his hands about four inches on each side. "About yay big. If it hasn't been preserved in a box, then you might be looking for something that's been pretty banged up over the years, decreasing its value significantly."

Lou pictured what Smitty was talking about. A display box would definitely help keep it in peak condition.

"I'll do a little more research about it today, see if anything's been sold in connection with a letter like this one." Smitty poked at the photocopy again. Lou could tell she'd just given the man something fun to keep him busy for a few hours.

"Thank you," Lou said. She waved and headed out the door to meet Cassidy.

Her nerves spiked higher than ever as she anticipated going inside the mansion. Now that she had confirmation that something valuable was inside the building at some point, it became even more real that it could've been the thing the killer was searching for and had returned for last night. The fact that she'd sent the police inside meant the killer probably hadn't found what they were looking for yet.

Lou recognized the danger in the way she'd thwarted the person's efforts twice, at that point. If she was right, and the killer really was searching for something valuable inside the mansion, the last person to stand in their way had wound up dead.

CHAPTER 19

Cassidy gulped as she and Lou stood in front of the mansion on Thread Lane.

"You okay?" Lou asked, checking on the woman standing next to her.

Cassidy nodded. "Fine. I need to get used to showing the place, so this will be good practice."

Lou shared in Cassidy's unease, and even though it was the middle of the day, a cloud of discontent floated above them as they walked forward and up to the front door. The porch groaned in complaint just as it had the day Lou had jogged up it after hearing the crash inside. But unlike her first visit, she and Cassidy entered through the front door, instead of wrapping around the porch to the back of the house where the kitchen was located.

The lock on the front door was old, though not requiring a large skeleton key as Lou had dramatically pictured in her mind. The door creaked as it swung open, making the porch sound downright quiet in comparison. It opened into a huge entryway with ceilings that must've vaulted up to at least twenty feet, enough to give an ornate chandelier room to hang.

Though it was covered in cobwebs and the metal wore a thick coating of dust, Lou could imagine that it had been beautiful back in the day. Intricate molding and wooden design elements covered the walls and ceilings alike. But everything had a weathered quality to it, like they were inside a photograph with a muddied filter layered over each surface.

Both Cassidy and Lou jumped when the door swung shut behind them with a slam.

"No wonder Ron thought this place was haunted," Lou said with a shiver, repeating Easton's sentiments from last night. "Everything makes noise and seems to act on its own."

"So ... what are you really here to look for?" Cassidy asked, her brown eyes sparkling.

A laugh almost bubbled out of Lou at her friend's eagerness, but any happiness felt wrong in the creepy house, especially after what had happened there just a week earlier. Lou wet her lips and turned to Cassidy.

"Smitty told me that the person who lived here prior to Ron was Rose Duncan." Lou checked with Cassidy, who nodded, before she continued. "Well, when Rose passed away thirty years ago, her daughter, Olivia, sold the house. They sold Smitty an old desk, among other items. Inside one drawer was a letter from a pocket-watchmaker to one of their relatives, probably a grandfather. Apparently, he'd saved this watchmaker guy's life in the First World War. To thank him, the watchmaker created a custom pocket watch. Smitty said it would've been worth at least a million."

Cassidy's eyes went wide. "Whoa."

"But they couldn't find it thirty years ago when they moved. I wonder if someone found out about it and thinks it could still be here." Lou scanned the space, her attention settling upstairs. That was where she'd seen the person in the window both times, so it was where she would start looking.

"Someone in the Duncan family?" Cassidy asked, squinting as if she were trying to think if she knew any of them.

Lou shrugged. "It could be one of them, or someone who knows the story. Heck, anyone who knows about that letter from the watchmaker would have an interest." She started up the ornate staircase.

"I wonder ..." Cassidy stopped at the bottom of the stairs.

Lou turned back toward her.

"It's just. The person who was interested in this place a few months ago. My assistant talked to them, not me." She frowned. "She told me the name, but it definitely wasn't one of the Duncans. I think I have it written down at the office. I've been meaning to call them now that the house is going to be on the market, but I've been busy with another sale."

"Good thinking," Lou said. "Maybe it's a family friend who learned about the watch and wanted the chance to come look." She continued on upstairs.

Even though the dark wood was scratched and worn, it was in better shape than the rest of the house. Lou's footsteps would've been deadened by the floral carpet lining the stairs, but the creaks and groans each one emitted made the sound-dampening effects of the carpet moot. Cassidy followed behind Lou.

"And you think whoever's been searching for the pocket watch killed Ronald?" Cassidy asked.

"It makes the most sense, given that I saw someone sneaking around the second floor the day Ron was murdered, and then again yesterday. Why would they ransack the house and continue to come back if their primary goal was to kill Ron?" Lou stopped at the first room she came to at the top of the landing.

The ornate glass doorknob creaked as Lou turned it and pushed the door open. Inside was a bed that held a mattress on a wooden bed frame, but there weren't any sheets or other decorations. An antique chair and a white-painted dresser sat on the other end of the room. Other than that, the room was empty.

Lou started with the dresser, opening the drawers, hunting for the special pocket watch. She looked out for anything in a wooden box after Smitty's assurance that something that expensive would've come in a container. Lou kept her eye out for other clues as well. Francine had mentioned a dusty place, and while the interior of the mansion was musty and covered in a layer of dust, Lou didn't feel like it could be the incredibly dusty place Francine had mentioned.

"So Ron might not have been killed by someone linked to the steel mill accident?" Cassidy asked, her voice breathy, as if she were going to need a moment to process that information.

Lou looked at her. "I mean, it's possible. I don't think it was anyone connected to the five people who died in the accident, but it could be someone who was injured or lost everything because of the accident or its aftermath. I haven't checked into anyone like that, other than Derrick."

Cassidy nodded, thoughts obviously buzzing through her mind. "I think you're right about this watch being the motivation. I mean, I know it was the twentieth anniversary of the accident, and there definitely are still people who aren't over what happened—like Derrick," she said, glancing at Lou. "But most of the county has moved on. If someone were going to kill Ron, I'd always expected it to be within the first few years."

"Right," Lou said. "And I just needed to come here and see for myself. The pocket-watch angle might be a dead end, but I wanted to try. Finding it might help us get one step closer to the killer."

Cassidy crossed her arms as Lou moved from the dresser to the bed. "But if the person who might be looking for the watch has been here multiple times, and still hasn't found it, what makes you think you're going to? I hear you're pretty detail oriented. Do you think that's going to help you?"

Lou smiled as she knelt next to the bed frame and ran her fingers along the wood. "You know what? I'm not sure. But I've interrupted the person twice, sending the police into the house. I also recently had a psychic reading, and the woman told me I would find the answers I was looking for here."

Cassidy adopted a smile to mimic Lou's. She let out a laugh. "Okay then. If we have a psychic behind us, let's get looking."

They went through another empty bedroom and a bathroom with no luck. Ronald hadn't done much decorating in any of those rooms, so it was easy to look through them, checking inside the few pieces of furniture. They were searching Ronald's room when Cassidy's phone rang, making them both jump.

"Whew, that scared me." Cassidy held a hand to her chest as she pulled her phone out of the purse on her shoulder. "Hey. What's up?" She held up a finger to Lou and stepped out into the hall.

Lou stood, frozen with indecision, inside Ronald's room. Clothes were tossed onto the large, sagging mattress. Dresser drawers were open, clothing spilling out of them. A wardrobe with mirrored doors hung open, the old silver backing distorting Lou's reflection. Ronald may have been messy, but this level of disorder had to have been caused by someone searching for something.

Lou wondered why all of Ronald's possessions were still there, but she figured whoever was buying the place—if anyone would want it—would have to clean out a lot or Cassidy had yet to get the place cleaned out.

"Okay, thanks. I'll get that right to you," Cassidy said, her voice coming back into focus as her high heels clicked closer.

Lou glanced over her shoulder in anticipation.

Cassidy poked her head into the room. She cringed. "Hey, I have to run back to the office for a few minutes and fax out a contract. I shouldn't be more than half an hour." She consulted her watch. "Do you want to stay here or come with me?"

"I'm fine hanging here," Lou said.

Cassidy nodded. "Okay, I'll be right back, I promise. Then we'll drive out to the horse show."

Lou waved and listened as Cassidy's heels clicked down the hallway. The house shuddered as the front door opened and closed, like it was letting out a long sigh. Lou focused on the room she was in.

As she took in the space, she shook her head. She wasn't going to find anything in here. The killer had obviously searched here already, likely first. What she needed to do was find a place they hadn't thought to look. Francine's words about dust and time swirled through Lou's head.

Moving back into the hallway, Lou scanned the space. Dust motes churned in the air, highlighted by the light spilling in through the tall, stained-glass window at the end of the hallway. She calmed her breathing, making her breaths slow and long. Her eyes moved along the hallway. The long rug that spanned the length of the hallway was askew at the end, and behind her, there was a chunk missing from the wall to the right of the top of the stairs, and one door had a newer brass handle instead of the old glass handles like the others. A few jagged pieces of ceramic chunks were scattered on the floor right next to the floorboard to the right of the hallway, underneath a small table. Dust layered over the top of the table, except for a ring in the middle.

Something had been there until recently. Lou thought of the crash she'd heard that day and the police saying they had found a broken vase on the landing at the top of the stairs. Walking over to the window, Lou glanced at the old glass and saw the sidewalk. That was the window she'd seen someone through both the day of the murder and yesterday.

So someone had been in the hallway. Lou had assumed it was Aiden, running downstairs and rushing away as she came inside. If the killer had still been here when Aiden came inside to find Ronald's body, maybe the sound of Aiden downstairs made the killer rush to hide?

Lou turned back to the small table. The killer must've run this way, bumping into the table and knocking over the vase. That's what she and Aiden had heard, that had made him run away and her run toward the house. She knelt and studied the broken remains that the police hadn't gathered.

But where had the killer gone from there? Maybe to the third floor, to the attic?

Based on the exterior windows, Lou knew there had to be an attic. She just didn't see a way to access it from the hallway.

Lou squinted at the room to the right, the bedroom she'd gone into first as she and Cassidy had searched. She scanned the ceiling, but there wasn't a drop ladder or access point for the attic. There also didn't seem like a place to hide in there, unless the person had slid under the bed. Lou craned her neck to check if the bed frame would even allow for such a thing.

She headed back out into the hallway, but something about the wooden decorative panel in the hallway caught her eye before she moved on. The wooden rosette in the middle of the panel didn't look like the one on the other side of the hallway. The center of this circle had a small gap around it, almost like a button. Lou pressed the wooden circle, and she heard something release, and the resistance behind her finger was gone.

A section of the panel about six feet tall and three feet wide moved toward her an inch as it released from whatever had been holding it in place. She moved aside the small table and kicked at the baseboard. The panel popped out a few inches farther. Lou pried the panel open the rest of the way with her fingers.

Stepping back, she peered into a dark passageway. It appeared to be a small walkway in between the two bedrooms, stopping about twenty feet ahead at the exterior wall of the house. Why would this small space be here?

Even if Lou couldn't tell what it was used for, it was clear that it had, in fact, been used. Dust! This definitely seemed more like what Francine had been talking about from her vision.

Footprints marred the otherwise dusty walkway in between the rooms. And unlike the star pattern from the soles of Aiden's shoes, Lou had a hunch these prints were from the footsteps of Ron's killer.

CHAPTER 20

Curiosity pulled Lou forward into the space between the two upstairs bedrooms in the Victorian mansion. While the ceiling above her was a good thirty feet high, the space was only about shoulder width, and she pulled her arms tight to her body as she stepped forward. She grabbed her phone and turned on the flashlight app, helping to illuminate the otherwise dark, dusty passageway.

Lou frowned, not sure it could be defined as a passageway actually. It didn't lead anywhere that she could see, stopping at the front exterior wall of the house.

Why would someone create a space here? To spy on the bedrooms? A shiver ran down her spine.

One thing was for sure. This was why the police hadn't found anyone the day of Ron's murder or yesterday when Lou had sent them looking. The person might've escaped, of course, but Lou felt it was even more likely that they were in the house, hiding the whole time, waiting for the police to leave. A coldness slid down Lou's back as she remembered the sound she'd heard when she was waiting for the police to show up last Friday. Maybe she really hadn't been alone. Had the killer still been in the house with her? It was finally time for some answers.

A text came through from Cassidy.

> Sorry. I need to get a contract out ASAP. I'll be a little longer.

Lou sent back a thumbs-up. She thought about texting about the secret passageway she'd found, but before she could, another text came through from Cassidy.

> Oh, I checked and the name of the person who was interested in buying the house about a month ago was Faith Wymer.

Lou paused. The name sounded familiar to her, but it had also been a long week. She couldn't quite place where she'd heard it before.

> Thanks for checking.

Lou was sure they would discuss it further when Cassidy returned.

Using her flashlight, Lou studied the walls to her right and left. The raw wood panels and beams used to construct the structure of the house and its rooms were all Lou could see. There wasn't a hole to be found, though, so the space wasn't for spying, as she'd first thought. She continued forward, toward the wall in front of her.

Lou held in a scream as her foot slipped, and she almost fell down a hole in the floor at the end of the passage, next to the exterior wall. Her hands flew out to brace herself. In the process, she let go of her phone and it spun in the air a few times before falling down the hole in the floor. It landed with a crack a moment later; the flashlight pointed up so it lit the opening it had fallen through. A cutout just big enough for an adult body took up the floor space next to the wall. Someone had created ladder rungs with pieces of wood, leading down to the first level of the house, where Lou's phone lay on what she really hoped wasn't concrete. That crack hadn't sounded pleasant, but the fact that her flashlight was still on gave her hope that her phone had survived the fall.

Lou peered down through the hole. *So it really was a passageway.*

A crashing sound came from somewhere behind Lou in the mansion. She froze and checked the time. Cassidy just said she was going to be a little longer. She wouldn't be back this soon. Also, Lou hadn't heard the front door open or shut. Lou flinched as another, louder crashing sound came from downstairs. Cassidy wouldn't be ransacking the house she was trying to sell.

Lou's heart stopped for a split second. Could it be the killer? Back to hunt for the treasure yet again?

Tiptoeing to the entrance of her hiding spot, Lou quietly pulled the panel shut. The light from her flashlight was too far back to help her much, but little pockets of sunlight streamed in from the hallway under the panel. In that dim light, Lou noticed a clasp she could latch on to the panel to hold it in place, the one that was pushed off the latch when she pressed the circle in the middle of the decorative rosette. She breathed easier for a moment, glad she'd located this hideaway instead of being caught out in the open, alone, by a potential killer.

That good feeling left her immediately as she remembered the killer likely knew about the passageway. And now she'd gone and shut herself inside it. If they found her in here and killed her, no one would know where she was or where to search.

Pressing her ear up to the panel she'd just closed, Lou

listened, hoping she could slip back out into the hall and find a different way out. But footsteps creaked up the ornate, old staircase, just as they had when Lou and Cassidy had walked up them. The person entered the bedroom to Lou's left and began opening and closing drawers, anger making their movements quick and powerful. The person moved from the bedroom to the hallway.

Their footsteps stopped on the other side of the panel.

Lou held her breath. She watched the circular piece of wood, willing it not to move. As she studied the mechanism, she realized the button wouldn't release the hook from the latch if she bent the metal hook in on itself. She reached for the hook with shaking fingers. Being careful not to make a sound, she used her fingers to bend the old piece of metal back on itself so it was more of a circle than a hook, and therefore couldn't be pushed off the latch. She wasn't sure if it would hold, but she didn't think the person could get in through this entrance anymore.

Which meant Lou needed to follow the passageway down to the lower level to get out.

The mysterious person's footsteps moved on, down the hallway, and Lou exhaled as quietly as she could. She turned back toward the hole in the floor, the light from her phone's flashlight still shining bright from below, and walked in slow, measured steps, careful not to make any noise. Lou tested each part of the wood floor before putting her total weight down, hoping to avoid any creaks or groans.

Blinking in the direct light of her flashlight, Lou turned around and climbed slowly down the hole in the floor, using the makeshift ladder. The wood pieces weren't deep enough for her toe, so she had to turn her feet sideways to make sure they didn't slip, all while trying not to make a noise. The process took a few minutes.

Lou was sweating and shaking by the time her foot found the floor. She stepped down, swiping her trembling hands over her face and taking a deep breath before retrieving her phone from the floor. While it was definitely wood, not concrete, it hadn't been kind to her poor phone. The screen was cracked and black. The flashlight must've stayed on since the app was already open, which meant it was likely just her screen that was broken.

As lucky as she felt at still having light in the dark passageway, Lou's heart raced at the realization that she couldn't text or call anyone for help. The safest thing would be to get out of the house and run to Cassidy's office down the street. Cassidy was also in danger if she came back to the mansion and came face-to-face with the killer.

Lou looked around. The passageway continued to her left and right. She was at a crossroads. One that might be the difference between life and death.

Moving to the left would take her to the living room she'd only glimpsed on the way in. That could be her safest bet, but it was in view of the staircase, so the killer might see her. To the right led toward the kitchen, where she'd been. She knew there was an exit that way, but it had also been where Ronald had been killed.

Lou was in a place where rational thinking wasn't helping. And since Francine's vision about the dust had panned out, Lou thought about the second vision she'd had. Time with a capital T was very important. Checking her watch, Lou saw it was twelve seventeen. She bit at her lip. The hour hand pointed straight ahead, toward the ladder she'd just climbed down. But the minute hand pointed to the right.

Was that the sign? Was her watch telling her which way to go?

Without a better idea, Lou followed it. She squared her

shoulders and tiptoed down the passageway to her right. As Lou moved farther down the passageway, it became clear that someone had spent quite a bit of time in this space. The area between studs on the interior wall held old paintings and magazine covers. There were a few from *Life* magazine, one from *Time* magazine, and another from *Popular Mechanics*. Newspaper clippings littered the space as well, but Lou didn't have time to give them more than a passing glance. Knick-knacks were lined up on the horizontal wood pieces, things Lou would've expected to see in Smitty's antique shop: old toys, glass figurines, and the occasional collectors glass.

The reminder of Smitty made something else click in Lou's mind. She remembered how she knew Faith Wymer.

She replayed the times Faith had come into the bookshop, all within the last month. She'd bought a book on pricing antiques, ordered another—which she'd picked up the other day—and had been looking for another that Lou hadn't been able to order. She'd referred Faith to talk to Lance Swatek or Smitty about the antiques about which she was searching for information.

Lou would've bet anything that the specific antique Faith was trying to find an evaluation on was a First World War-era personalized pocket watch.

There wasn't a pocket watch—alone or in a wooden box— among the items, however. A bottle of perfume made Lou pause. She would've bet anything that it was the dusty-rose scent that Ronald had complained about and Aiden had smelled the day he'd found Ron's body.

Between that and the sounds of someone creeping around inside the walls of the old house, Lou guessed that would account for Ronald thinking the house was haunted. Faith had been the ghost, though Lou did not know how the woman would've had time to discover the secret passageways in the house if Ron was always home. But that was a question to answer later once she was safely away from the mansion.

Lou studied the walls as she walked but kept the goal of escape at the forefront of her mind. She could always come back and examine the items in more detail once she'd gotten away with her life. She wouldn't be able to do anything if she were dead.

The passageway stopped after what seemed like a mile but was probably only forty feet. A three-foot-square piece of wood sat on the floor at the end of the passageway. When Lou crouched next to it, she found it was latched with a simple hook on this side, like the panel upstairs. Lou checked the floor, but there were no other passageways down. Forward was her only option.

Pressing her ear up to the board, Lou listened for any sounds. Hearing nothing, she quietly unlatched the hook, and let the door swing toward her. The space beyond the makeshift door was also dark, but Lou flashed her light and noticed that the space was filled with macaroni and cheese boxes, jars of spaghetti sauce, and canned soups. All the things Aiden mentioned buying each week for Ronald. This was a pantry.

Lou crouched and crawled through the opening. She didn't even bother closing the passageway door behind her. After performing the same listening routine at the pantry door, Lou opened the door into the kitchen, her heart in her throat. Sticking her broken phone in her back pocket, Lou pushed on the pantry door. When it creaked open, she peered out to the left and right.

She was in the kitchen. And she was alone.

But as Lou stepped out of the pantry, someone else entered the kitchen too. Fear pulsed through Lou's body as she recognized the person.

CHAPTER 21

Ascream peeled out of Lou as her gaze fell on Faith Wymer.

Faith took another step, standing in the exact spot Ronald's body had lain.

Lou's mind flicked through her options, but as Faith's face flashed with recognition, Lou got an idea. Faith didn't know what Lou suspected about her involvement in Ron's murder.

Pulling all of her energy into the acting job of her life, Lou let out a laugh and leaned forward.

"Omigosh, Faith! You almost gave me a heart attack." Lou patted her chest. "Cassidy said there might be other buyers looking at the house today, but I definitely thought I was alone."

Faith's worried face morphed into relief. "I scared *you*? What about you jumping out of the pantry like that?" She shook her head.

"So you're interested in the place too?" Lou asked, trying to sound conversational, even though the only thing she wanted to do was run.

Faith studied the room. "I am, actually. This is my grandmother's old house. When my mom inherited it thirty years ago, I'd just gotten married, and I wasn't in a place where I could purchase it, but I miss the place, so I thought I'd take a look." She shrugged.

Lou had been right. Faith's maiden name was Duncan, and if her grandmother used to own the house, Lou bet that's how she knew about the secret passageways. The reminder of the passageway made Lou all the more aware that she'd left the low crawl space door open in the pantry. From where Faith stood, she wouldn't be able to see the open passageway exit, but if she took a step forward, she'd have a clear view of it. As much as Lou itched to close the pantry door behind her, she knew it would look suspicious. She couldn't risk it.

"Oh man. If this was your family's house, you should totally buy it. I was just looking." Lou waved a dismissive hand. "My late husband used to love Victorian houses, and we'd always talked of getting one someday. But this is obviously meant for you." Lou laughed nervously. "I'll leave you to it." She edged toward the back sliding glass door, the one she'd come through the day she'd found Ronald's body.

"Don't let me chase you off." Faith stepped forward, holding out a hand. "I'm still not one hundred percent ..." Her gaze flicked into the open pantry.

Lou could tell the moment she saw the open passageway door, because Faith's expression darkened.

It appeared to take some effort, but Faith pulled her mouth back into a smile. "And how'd you find out about the secret passageways?" Now she scanned Lou as if searching for something. The watch, no doubt.

Lou scratched at her cheek nervously. "I notice details. It's nothing."

Faith swallowed. "Is it? I tried opening the entrance upstairs, and it wouldn't budge. What did you do to it?" She held Lou's gaze, and her own flicked to the knife block next to her on the counter.

Lou's cheeks flushed hot. Was this how it had happened with Ronald? Did Faith stand here with him, threatening him before stabbing him?

"I'd better—" Lou pointed behind her feebly.

Faith narrowed her eyes. "You're not going anywhere."

Lou swallowed.

"Details, huh?" Faith rested her hand on the counter next to the knife block. "So you figured out what I was looking for, then?"

"I don't know what you're ..." Lou's voice cracked with fear and petered out as she saw Faith wasn't buying it. "The pocket watch," Lou said.

Faith's eyes flashed with anger at the words. "I know it's here somewhere." She slammed her hand onto the counter. "It's mine. He was trying to keep it from me."

Lou jumped. "So you killed him?" she ventured.

Faith's whole body tensed. She pointed at Lou. "It was a mistake. He was to blame, really." Her finger shook with anger, and she let her hand drop to her side. "I didn't know he was in the kitchen. I was trying to slip out unnoticed, like I had been for weeks, but he caught me." She sneered. "He picked up the knife and lunged at *me*." She placed a hand on her chest. "I was just trying to get away from him, but he tried to stab me." Her icy demeanor fell, a lip quivering before she said, "And so I turned the knife on him."

Lou's heartbeat increased, and her pulse pounded in her ears. Something creaked in the hallway. Did the ghost really exist? No, that had been Faith the whole time.

"You were the ghost," Lou said, not even a hint of a question in her voice.

Faith nodded, her smile returning. "I came to that miserable man and told him that my family used to own this place, that I was looking for something of my grandmother's." She scowled. "He told me to get off his property. Luckily, we used to come stay with my grandma for a week every Christmas when we were children. Not only did I learn about the secret passageways, but I also knew how to get in and out of the house unnoticed, using a window that doesn't lock. So I came back, snuck inside, and searched on my own."

"And you sprayed perfume?" Lou asked.

Faith laughed. "To mess with him. The poor fool thought he was hearing a ghost. The perfume only made him more sure."

"But you didn't find what you were looking for." Lou shifted her weight. "Why didn't you tell anyone? You could've had the police help you search the house. If the pocket watch is legally yours. And it sounds like you were only using self-defense when you killed Ronald."

She bit her lip. "Because the watch isn't legally mine. It's my sister's. My mom passed away and left it to her, even though they could never find it. My sister doesn't care. She lives in a big house with her perfect husband. Meanwhile, my husband kicked me out of our house, wants a divorce, and I need the money."

Lou bit her lip, trying to think of a way out of the house. Faith might not have stabbed Ron on purpose, but her hand was too close to the knife block on the counter for Lou's comfort.

Another creak sounded in the hallway.

Faith's eyes darted nervously to her right, toward the sound. Just then, something crashed near the front door. Faith turned to look, but Lou took the opportunity to run. She bolted for the back door. Faith yelled for her to stop, her voice ripping through the house, but Lou was already out the sliding door and running.

She thought about following Aiden's route through the trees, but the fear of getting lost in the forest with a killer was too great. She needed to go where there were people.

Taking a hard right, Lou ran along the side of the house, heading for Thread Lane, for people.

She'd only gotten a few yards when she ran into someone.

Her breath left her, whether from the impact or fear, for just a moment before she realized the arms surrounding her were strong and warm. A beard scratched against her forehead.

"Ben?" Lou breathed, confused and disoriented. Maybe she hadn't survived. Maybe she hadn't really gotten away.

Hands wrapped around her upper arms, and a face came into view.

A dark beard came into focus first, but then green eyes met with hers. Not Ben's deep-brown ones.

"Noah." His name came out 90 percent exhalation as she let herself lean into him.

She'd never noticed how much Noah was like Ben until that moment. They were so very different in personality that it never seemed right to compare them, but Lou could see it in that moment.

"Lou, are you okay?" His deep voice rumbled through his chest.

"Call the police," she said, her voice croaking. "Faith killed Ron." When he didn't move, she stepped back, looking up at him.

"Oh, I heard everything. I called. They're already here." Noah smiled and gestured to the police parked out front, swarming the building.

"How ...?" Between the adrenaline and fear surging through her veins, Lou couldn't seem to get a full sentence out.

"Cassidy called me. She got stuck at the office and asked if I'd drive you to the horse show and pick up Marigold," Noah explained. "I was just walking up to the front door when I heard you scream. I snuck inside and listened to the conversation. When it became apparent you were in trouble, I texted for Cassidy to call the police and made noise to distract Faith so you could get away."

Lou's mouth tipped up on one side. That was a very Noah thing to do. Ben would've come in, all loud and intimidating. Noah was quieter. That must have been why she'd never seen their similarities before.

After being so scared, it felt odd to be safe, to be okay. Lou sank to a seated position in the grass just as a police officer walked over to see if they were okay.

"We're good." Noah held up a hand. "I think she just needs a minute." He glanced down at Lou. "Or ten. Maybe just wait until Easton gets here from Silver Lake. That should be enough time."

Somehow, Noah's calmness was rubbing off on Lou. She backed away. "Wait, why is Easton in Silver Lake?" Her eyes went wide. "The horse show!" Lou got to her feet.

"Willow's truck wouldn't start this morning, so Easton used his to tow OC to the show for her," Noah said.

"Can I borrow your phone?" Lou asked, pulling out hers to show the busted screen and flashlight that was stuck on.

Noah handed his over, looking unsure of what to do as she gave him hers in exchange.

She dialed Willow's number, one of the few phone numbers she knew by heart, the same one Willow had since they were in college.

"It's me. It's Lou," she said into the phone when Willow answered. "I'm fine. I'm okay."

She knew Easton rushing off would've scared her friend and her nieces to death, not to mention the fact that they wouldn't be able to get ahold of her.

A tremendous gust of breath came through the other end of the line. "Ohthankgoodness." It was all one word. "She's okay, girls. I'm talking to her now. You scared us, Lou. Easton ran off, saying something about you and the killer in the mansion together. He said Noah was with you, but I didn't know if you were safe." Willow's words came out too fast, and Lou guessed she was pacing back and forth as she spoke on the phone. "I'm putting you on speaker."

There was a scraping sound, and then Lou heard her nieces talking all at once.

"Auntie Lou, we were so worried about you."

"We were so scared."

Their voices were jumbled together, so she couldn't tell who said what.

"Hi, Lou." That small voice was definitely Marigold's.

She swallowed. "Hi, everyone. I'm okay. Everything's okay, and I'll tell you the entire story when I get to the horse show soon."

Willow scoffed, "You don't have to come, Lou."

Lou scoffed back, "Of course I'm coming. I might miss your first class because I have to give my statement and make sure I'm cleared to leave, but I'm going to be there cheering you and OC on. I want to see you win it all."

Willow laughed. "Okay, we'll see you soon. Love you."

The girls chimed in at the same time again. "Yes. Love you, Auntie Lou."

Heart full, Lou hung up the call and looked at Noah. She heaved out a sigh as she handed him his phone.

"What are you smiling at?" she asked him.

He scratched at his cheek to hide his grin. Shaking his head, he said, "You're a good friend, Louisa Henry. One of the better ones I've ever met, I'd say."

Lou elbowed him, feeling normal again now that she'd

talked to Willow and the girls. "You should talk, Noah Ramero. You're a pretty good friend to have around, especially when a girl needs saving ... and veterinary care for her many cats," she added at the end.

Noah wrapped an arm around her shoulders, and they started walking toward the grouping of police cruisers. "Speaking of cats, I hear we have an interested adopter for the Artful Clawdger."

Lou frowned. "I wanted you to check, though, to make sure they're safe. That last one got me all worried."

Noah nodded. "Two names on the do-not-adopt-to list in one week would be quite the *twist*, don't you think?" He prodded her with an elbow. "See what I did there? Twist? I thought you might've *missed* it." He shot her a big grin.

Lou chuckled. "Yes, *Oliver Twist*. I see."

What she saw even clearer was the police leading Faith out of the house in handcuffs. Noah had been trying to distract her with puns. She focused on him, not the woman who'd let her obsession with finding a long-lost treasure lead her to taking a life.

"I would come up with a better rhyme, but I don't have much time," Lou said. But before Noah could say anything else, Lou sucked in a breath. "*Time*," she said. "Time with a capital T." Her eyes flashed up to Noah's. "I know where the pocket watch is."

Easton climbed out of a taxi, his hair a mess, his eyes wild. They settled on Lou and Noah. He raced over. "I couldn't get the truck unhitched from the trailer in time, so I called a cab. What are you smiling about, Lou?"

She pressed her lips together. "Follow me. I have something to show you. We're going to want to call Smitty. He'll know what to do with it."

CHAPTER 22

Louisa woke early on Sunday morning to find two teenage girls asleep, one on either side of her in bed. They must've climbed in with her at some point during the night, despite her protestations that she was fine after her run-in with a murderer. But from the way they clung to her upon her arrival at the horse show, she should've known they wouldn't let her out of their sight for long.

She stretched in bed, a smile on her face as she thought of finding the pocket watch. It had been tucked in a small cubby in the wall, hidden by the *Time* magazine cover.

Francine had been right. Lou would have to make a trip to Brine to thank the psychic.

Smitty said it definitely looked like the watch in the letter he'd found. Easton had already contacted Faith's sister to let her know the pocket watch had been located, so it looked like it was going to be in the Duncan family's hands once again.

Lou's grin grew wider as she thought of Willow waking up with the grand champion ribbon hanging in her bedroom. She and OC had nailed their dressage test, and Lou couldn't have been prouder. But that was nothing compared to the excitement Lou felt at what she'd accidentally glimpsed as she was searching for Willow after the ribbon ceremony.

She'd seen Willow and Easton kissing behind the horse trailer. Lou couldn't wait to ask her friend all about it. She needed every detail but figured Willow hadn't told her because of her run-in with a murderer and the impending anniversary.

Right. Lou's happiness faltered as she remembered what day it was. Sunday. The one-year anniversary of Ben's death. Lou looked at her nieces as she waited for the gut punch that she knew would follow the thoughts of the anniversary. But moments later, she was still waiting. It didn't come.

The ache that she carried around inside of her was still there, but it was as if Lou's body couldn't process the awful gut-wrenching grief while she was surrounded by such love.

Maddy blinked awake. "Morning," she said through a yawn.

"Morning." Lou reached forward and affectionately tucked an errant strand of dark hair behind Maddy's ear. "How'd your dad react to the news last night?"

The girls had called Joe and Emily, talking until late. Lou had tried to stay up and wait, but she was beat from the day and must've fallen asleep.

Maddy nodded. "Good."

"They said to say hi, and tell you they're glad you're okay," Mia said, stretching as she sat up.

Lou cringed. "I hope they let you come back after hearing everything that went down this week."

"We weren't even close by when things got dangerous," Maddy scoffed as if she was angry she'd been left out.

"Yeah," Mia said, "And Dad's been super open since ..." She fiddled with the sheets.

Maddy picked up where her sister left off. "She's right. He used to think we were going to get hurt and wouldn't let us go anywhere with our friends if he couldn't track us the whole time. But now, he keeps saying things like 'Life is short. Have fun!' and rarely says no when we ask him to go places."

Lou understood the sentiment. She, too, had felt a level of reckless abandon after Ben's death. He'd done everything right. He was healthy. The man probably ran the equivalent of a marathon each week. They watched what they ate and only had the occasional drink. He was careful—he never put himself in dangerous situations. Despite all that, a heart attack had taken him from them too soon.

She wondered if her recent sleuthing tendencies were in response to this injustice. Why worry about putting herself in danger if danger could find you even when you were careful?

Lou wrapped an arm around each of her niece's and hugged them close. "I love you two. I'm so sorry Ben's not here to see you grow up into the lovely women you are becoming."

The girls laid a head on each shoulder, and one of them sniffed.

"He can see us. I think so, anyway," Mia said in a small voice.

"I do too." Lou planted a kiss on Mia's forehead, then Maddy's. "Okay, what do you say we get this day started?"

The girls smiled, and they all climbed out of bed.

Willow showed up a little while later with coffees and pastries from the Bean and Button. "Put me to work. I'm a bookshop employee today."

They needed all hands on deck. It was hopping just like Saturday morning, if not more.

George showed up before they even opened, pulling Lou into a tight hug that almost reminded her of one of Willow's. Silas and Forrest stopped by to make sure Lou was okay, along with half the town—though Lou suspected that many of them were searching for gossip.

Derrick showed up, ready for a new Louis L'Amour novel.

Apparently, Easton let him off with a warning for lying about his alibi. He was all smiles and even thanked Lou for helping him get that secret off his chest.

"You have no idea how much energy it was taking for me to keep that to myself for so long," he said as she rang up the book.

Noah and Marigold came in around lunchtime.

"I had a minute, and I thought I'd check that application you mentioned." Noah smiled and waved at the nieces. He'd met them yesterday at the horse show, and he and Maddy had chatted about veterinarian school for a good hour.

Lou grabbed the paperwork she'd saved. She handed over the application, saying, "I'm not sure if it matters. I haven't heard from her again since I told her to check back in, just like the other woman. Maybe they're working together?"

Noah frowned at the application. "I don't recognize this name. Let me run it by Kathleen again."

"It'll be too bad if she doesn't come back. It was nice to see Clawdger getting the attention he deserves," Lou thought aloud.

Noah chuckled. "It looks like he's getting someone's attention now." Noah gestured toward Clawdger and Purrt Vonnegut.

The two male cats were seated on the couch together, snuggled into a cat sandwich and cleaning each other. Both of them were purring so loud, Lou could hear it from across the shop.

"That's adorable. I haven't seen them do that before." Lou covered her mouth with her hand.

"They're like best friends." Mia walked over, scrunching up her shoulders as she took in the adorable sight.

"Kathleen says that name isn't on any of our lists," Noah reported as he checked his phone. He scanned the paper and added, "Everything looks great to me as well."

Lou nodded. "Okay, maybe I was just being paranoid.

Though, I think it's a good thing she hasn't shown up again, because now Clawdger seems to be part of a bonded pair."

Noah agreed and walked over to talk with Maddy. Lou couldn't help but watch the two of them as they chatted. Maddy used to have a really special bond with Ben, and the way she laughed and stared up at Noah—like he was her idol—it was almost like seeing that again. But it could also just be Lou being sentimental because of what day it was.

A customer burst into the shop, stealing Lou's attention away from her niece and Noah. Lou blinked as she recognized Peggy Olson. The woman's hair was wild, her eyes large as she scanned the place until she located Lou.

"Tell me you haven't given her away yet," Peggy said, her voice clawing forward like a desperate hand.

"Miss Clawvisham-er-Peaches?" Lou pointed over to the couch, where the beautiful cat lounged with Marigold. "No, she's still here."

Peggy's chin trembled like she might cry from relief. "It was the fleas. My son, Brian, he was itchy because of the fleas, not because he was allergic to the cat."

Lou frowned. "I left you a message about it almost a week ago. What took you so long?"

Peggy grimaced. "I'm not very good at checking my messages. And when Brian didn't get better after Peaches left, I started calling in to get him appointments at the doctor's office and with an allergist." She cleared her throat. "The doctor recognized the flea bites on his skin right away. I spent most of the weekend deep cleaning my house to get rid of the bugs. I didn't listen to your message until this morning."

Lou waved a hand to dismiss Peggy's worries. "That's okay. So you want her back?"

"Can we do that?" Peggy's voice was so hopeful it almost broke Lou's heart.

"Of course. She was your cat in the first place, and I know she'll have a loving home." Lou smiled as she noticed Noah watching them from across the room. "But I will say, I would recommend taking her in to see a real veterinarian. I don't know who the breeder was that you bought her from, but they obviously didn't tell you she was infested with fleas, so I'm not sure if I'd trust them on keeping her up to date on her medical needs."

Peggy nodded emphatically. "I'll let Noah know I'll be in to make an appointment this week." She raced over to him, eliciting a huge grin from the veterinarian as she reached him.

A little while later, Peggy left with Peaches—in a crate this time, instead of holding the cat in her arms—and an appointment with Noah at the clinic that week. Lou had felt how much Peggy had loved that cat when she'd dropped her off and was glad it worked out.

Speaking of working out, just before closing that day, the red-haired woman came back for the Artful Clawdger. Apparently, she'd stopped by yesterday, but it had been during the afternoon when Lou had closed the shop. She was very motivated to adopt Clawdger still, and when Maddy and Mia mentioned how close he'd gotten to Purrt Vonnegut—despite Lou's nonverbal cues not to say anything—she'd told them she had always wanted two cats. So both Purrt and Clawdger got to go home with her.

After they closed the shop for the day, Lou, Maddy, Mia, and Willow settled onto the couches in the bookstore. Sapphire was fast asleep between Maddy and Mia. Anne Mice was purring away in Lou's lap, and even Catnip Everdeen was crouched on the back of Willow's chair. Lou had gone from six felines to three so quickly, her head spun. But she knew more cats would come. The ones who needed a safe, cozy place to stay while people out there searched for them would always have a home at Whiskers and Words.

Willow passed around cups and poured them all sparkling cider. She held her glass up and said, "To Benjamin Henry."

Tears crowded Lou's eyes as she raised her glass and said, "To Ben."

The girls did the same, and then the four of them sipped at their cider and told their favorite stories of the larger-than-life man who'd left such a hole in their lives when he'd left too early.

When the cider was gone and they'd shed many tears—and just as much laughter—Lou glanced over at Willow.

"Okay, is it the right time to bring up how I caught Easton giving Willow a kiss after she won her class yesterday?" Lou asked, a smirk forming as her best friend's eyes widened.

"Louisa Henry!" Willow squeaked, but it was drowned out by the teenage girls cheering and jumping over to hug their honorary aunt.

"We knew it!" Maddy said after they were done squealing, making a fuss, and scaring away all the cats.

Mia nodded smugly.

Willow rolled her eyes. "He was just congratulating me on my win."

Lou and the girls sent each other skeptical looks. Then they all burst into laughter.

CHAPTER 23

A WEEK LATER …

Lou hugged Mia and Maddy so tight, she was approaching "Willow hug" tightness. They squeaked in surprise and then laughed, moving on to get another too-tight hug from Willow.

The airport was bustling, even at six in the morning. It was one thing Lou loved about airports: time didn't have the same meaning inside their walls. Hours could go by in a flash if you were late for a flight. Or a layover could feel like days. She hoped her nieces experienced only on-time flights and clear skies on their trip back to Montana.

"I love you so much," Lou said, beaming at the young women in front of her.

This trip had really shown her how much they'd grown up. Before she knew it, they would finish high school and branch out on their own.

"We love you too," the girls said in unison.

"Both of you," Mia said to Willow, who stood taller in response.

"We'll text when we get through security." Maddy checked her phone as if she worried it might've stopped working in the last few minutes.

"And when you get on the plane, and when you land," Willow instructed.

Lou held back a chuckle. Willow had become an overprotective aunt in the course of two weeks. Lou sent a discreet wink at Maddy to let her know to humor Willow. It wasn't that she didn't trust the girls or believe they couldn't handle themselves. It was purely a demonstration of love and caring so greatly for someone who wasn't by your side.

Once they were back in the car, Lou sighed. "Good visit," she said.

Willow nodded, though she kept her eyes on the road. "Those nieces of yours are pretty special."

Lou smiled. "They sure are."

"Persuasive," Willow said, wrinkling her nose.

Lou laughed. "Yep." She glanced at Willow, who was still making a thinking face. "What? Are you finally ready to admit that they were right about your feelings for Easton? Because you were totally kissing him back last week."

Willow pressed her lips together. "No, the kissing was good. Easton's good." She shot a girlish smile over at Lou, but then she was back to watching the road and frowning.

"So what? What else did the girls say to you?" Lou asked, growing concerned.

"It was them, but also Francine, the psychic, and you," Willow explained. "You took a leap and did something scary, something you didn't know would work out. You followed your heart."

Lou studied her best friend for a moment, and then she sucked in a breath. "You're not talking about ...?"

Willow nodded. "My dream of opening my own nursery. I

mentioned it to the girls on our way to the show, and they wouldn't drop the idea. They said it was just like what Francine had told me about holding myself back from the things I've always wanted. And as much as I love teaching, that nursery has been my dream for—"

"Since we were nine?" Lou squinted one eye as she thought back. Happiness expanded through her chest. "I think it's a fantastic idea." She grabbed Willow's free hand and squeezed tight. "And I'll be there by your side every step of the way."

Willow squeezed back, and they drove back to the small town of Button, home.

WHISKERS AND WORDS WILL RETURN ...

Pick up the fourth book in the series.

Could Lou be falling right into the killer's trap?

Louisa's first fall in Button is everything she hoped it would be: corn mazes, pumpkin patches, quirky town traditions, and beautiful foliage. The only unexpected thing: a dead body found in a pile of fall leaves.

When Lou starts getting clues about the murder, she's wary, to say the least. Are the clues from the murderer, baiting her into a trap? Or are they from someone who truly wants to help? Keeping the clues a secret from the police may be the only way to ensure she continues to receive them, but it could also get Lou in deep trouble with the law, if not worse: dead.

Buy now!

Join Eryn Scott's mailing list to learn about new releases and sales!

Also by Eryn Scott

A Murder at the Morrisey Mystery Series

Ongoing series * Friendly ghosts * Quirky downtown Seattle building

Pebble Cove Teahouse Mysteries

Completed series * Friendly ghosts * Oregon Coast * Cat mayors

PEPPER BROOKS COZY MYSTERY SERIES

Completed series * Literary mysteries * Sweet romance * Cute dog

STONEYBROOK MYSTERIES

Ongoing series * Farmers market * Recipes * Crime solving twins * Cats!

Whiskers and Words Mysteries

Ongoing series * Best friends *
Bookshop full of cats

About the Author

Eryn Scott lives in the Pacific Northwest with her husband and their quirky animals. She loves classic literature, musicals, knitting, and hiking. She writes cozy mysteries and women's fiction. Join her mailing list to learn about new releases and sales!

www.erynscott.com

Made in the USA
Middletown, DE
05 October 2023

40060931R00130